The Diaries of Ay'esha
Trapped and Trained

First Edition

Published by The Nazca Plains Corporation
Las Vegas, Nevada
2008

ISBN: 978-1-934625-23-1

Published by

The Nazca Plains Corporation ®
4640 Paradise Rd, Suite 141
Las Vegas NV 89109-8000

PUBLISHER'S NOTE
The Diaries of Ay'esha is a work of fiction created wholly by *Charles Forbin's* imagination. All characters are fictional and any resemblance to any persons living or deceased is purely by accident. No portion of this book reflects any real person or events.

Cover Photo, Mitchel Evans
Art Director, Blake Stephens

The Diaries of Ay'esha
Trapped and Trained

First Edition

Published by The Nazca Plains Corporation
Las Vegas, Nevada
2008

The Diaries of Ay'esha
Trapped and Trained

First Edition

Charles Forbin

CONTENTS

I

I awoke to a flare of light. Where was I? I tried to roll over and discovered my hands were bound. I tried to take a deep breath and found I was gagged, as well.

The last thing I remembered was stopping to help a young woman change a tire. I had bent over to turn the tire wrench, and then… blackout.

I didn't have a headache, so I hadn't been hit on the head, but my thoughts were fuzzy. Drugged, perhaps. Why? I wasn't anyone special, not worth kidnapping or even robbing, for that matter.

I was dragged into the light and ordered to stand. The light was blinding, so I could not clearly see my captor.

"Walk ahead of me. Do not turn around, or you will be corrected!"

Corrected? A woman's voice. The young woman with the flat tire? I was directed down a hallway and into a room and ordered to lie on a table, face down. I started to resist and felt a sharp slash of pain across my ass. I realized for the first time that I was naked.

"Now, lie down, or I will increase the pain."

I lay down on the table as I was ordered. My legs were tied to the table, and then my waist was secured, as well. My hands were gripped strongly and untied. I started to lash out and was promptly subjected to a further sample of pain.

My hands were tied to the table, and I felt a hand run down my spine and lower until I felt the hand touch my genitals. A finger gently probed my ass.

"You are here for a specific purpose. You are to be examined for your usefulness. If are found useful, then you will be trained to serve us. If not, you will be dispensed with."

That sounded ungodly.

"You will now be tested for your pain tolerance."

I heard her walk away. There was a long wait, and I had almost dropped off to sleep again when...*thwack!* I tried to leap up, but the restraints held firm.

"I see I have your attention," said the voice. "Now we will proceed to test your ability to withstand pain."

I felt something like tape being placed onto parts of my body.

"The sensors will record your reaction to pain stimuli. I will observe your reaction. I will decide when you have had enough. You may try to scream if you like, but the gag is quite secure, and no one will hear you."

The first whip strokes were firm, but not terribly painful. They increased and changed location. The pain increased in intensity. The pain grew as the location of the strokes changed. My breathing became more and more labored as the strokes became harder.

Suddenly, they stopped.

A gentle hand stroked my head and wiped away the tears. "An excellent beginning. You have done well. Rest, now. We will begin again soon."

A blindfold was placed over my eyes, as I passed into an exhausted sleep.

When I awoke, I was still on the table, but now I was on my back, still restrained and blindfolded. My legs were raised in the air, exposing my ass. I waited, fearful of what might be next. What use could I be to this woman? Why had I been chosen?

Soon I heard the Voice again.

"I see you are awake now. If you will agree to remain silent until I give you permission to speak, I will remove the gag. If you agree to this, nod your head."

I nodded as well as I could.

She removed the gag, and I gasped.

"If you would like some water, nod your head."

I nodded again and felt the nipple of a baby bottle placed in my mouth. I sucked greedily until the nipple collapsed. It was withdrawn.

"Now, we will proceed with the next series of pain tests. I will also evaluate your holding capacity."

Holding capacity?

The tape was applied again, and the pain started as before. Suddenly, I felt a sharp pain on my left nipple, followed by an identical pain on my right.

"These nipple clamps can be adjusted tightly enough to pierce your nipples, if desired. I wish to see if the pain of your nipples will distract you from pain in other areas."

The pain of the whipping increased. The pain in my nipples was constant. I soon drifted into a stupor from the whipping. It even began to feel pleasant in a strange way. Suddenly, the pressure was released from my nipples. The blood surged back into them. I opened my mouth to scream and was gagged again, changing the scream into a gurgle.

"You were not given permission to speak. I consider screaming speaking. You will be corrected for that mistake."

There was a pause, then a burning pain on my chest that made me moan into the gag.

"You will not make that error again, will you?"

I shook my head weakly.

The gag was removed.

"Now, we begin the holding capacity test. You will be removed to a pen following this test. You will find food and water there. Do you understand me? You may speak as a dog. One bark for 'yes', and two for 'no'."

I barked once.

"Good. Would you like the blindfold removed?"

I barked in the affirmative.

"If you do well on the test, I will remove it."

There was a pause, and I heard the snap of a rubber glove being pulled on. Then, I felt coldness on my asshole and a probing finger. I tensed, and then slowly relaxed as the probing finger withdrew.

"Test begins."

I felt my asshole widen and then felt something being shoved into it. It penetrated deeper into my bowels until I felt like I was going to explode. I felt the urge to piss from the pressure. I had never been penetrated before by something that long.

I started cramping from the pressure and the pain. The pressure continued for what seemed like an eternity, and then whatever the item was, it was withdrawn slowly. The final removal caused me to gasp in pain, followed by relief.

The blindfold was removed, and for the first time I saw my tormentor.

It was the girl from the car. She was dressed in a black corset, studded belt and high leather boots. Her manner was imperious, but her tone was gentle. She shook back the dark hair that had cascaded over her face and removed the rubber gloves from her hands.

"You will be released from your bonds, and I will take you to the holding pen." She indicated the leather quirt hanging from her belt. "Any attempt to escape, and you will be corrected. Is that clear to you?"

I barked once. I desired my freedom, but I knew that I could not escape from her. Her voice held me in its grip, almost as tightly as did the bonds. What was happening to me? I felt helpless in her presence.

As she released the bonds, I felt uncertain, even fearful of her. But she was just a young woman. Why the fear? Was it the torture? I was a man; I should be able to take control from her. But I found as she looked at me, my will to resist was slowly slipping away.

She knew it and smiled, a sly knowing smile, holding only the promise of future abuse for me. "Get up and walk ahead of me. I want your head down. Do not speak to anyone who may speak to you. Until I give you permission to speak, you are to act as if you are mute. Nod if you understand this order."

I nodded quickly.

"Good. Start walking. Through the door and turn right. Stop when I tell you to."

I walked out the door and turned right as directed. A few feet later, the order to stop was given.

In front of me was a large metal cage.

"Open the door and get in."

I started to turn towards her and felt the slash of the quirt across my back.

"Enter the pen, now!"

I opened the door and crawled inside. The pen was just big enough to turn in, but not large enough to stretch out or to sit upright. The floor was padded with a plastic mat. A large water bottle, like one used in laboratories, was mounted against the side of the cage.

The door was locked behind me, and a food dish was slid into a slot in the side of the cage next to the water bottle. In it were scraps of meat and vegetables, a piece of bread and some fruit.

"You may eat any time you are ready," she said. "I will return later to cover your pen for the night."

With that, she turned and left the room, leaving me caged like an animal, wondering what our next encounter might bring.

II

She returned some time later and placed a cover over my cage after removing the empty food dish, not speaking to me. I curled up in the darkness and pondered the sudden change in my life. I was caged like a lab rat, or perhaps like a canary. I had a sudden wild urge to sing "I'm only a bird in a gilded cage." But, I fought it back. I had been ordered not to speak. How would she know if I did? I couldn't be sure that she wouldn't know.

The question of "why" still dogged me. And the types of tests confused me. Why was I being tortured? How would I be found useful? Or, not useful? And trained to serve whom? She had said "trained to serve us." Her? Someone else? Perhaps this was some kind of strange dream. Perhaps I had been hit by a car while helping the girl change her tire and was in a hospital. The Wizard of Oz had nothing on this dream... if it were a dream.

Her voice came from above, startling me. "You can't escape by clicking the heels of your ruby slippers three times."

I must have said it out loud. She had been listening. Now what?

"You should sleep now. I will correct you in the morning after your feeding and your walk."

I tried to sleep, but sleep wouldn't come easily. But come it did, like fog on little cat feet, it crept over my mind leaving me in a black void.

I awoke to the feel of a stream of warm water playing over my body. My bladder emptied in response and soaked the floor of the pen with my piss. The warm water continued until the pen was clean.

I looked up to see the young woman dressed in a lab coat holding a hose. "Your correction has been postponed. I will bring your morning ration,"

She returned with the food pan filled with warm oatmeal. "Eat."

I placed my face in the pan and lapped up the warm food as well as I could. When I looked up again, she was watching me. No, studying me would be a better term. I started watching her in return.

She smiled at me. "You have spirit. And you have questions. Are you afraid of me? You may speak."

I hesitated. Was I afraid of her? No, not of her, but just her power over me. "I am not afraid of you. I am afraid of what you might do to me."

"A wise answer; you may ask one question."

A single question. I thought furiously. If I could ask the right question, it would provide the answer to others. "What is the purpose of these tests you are performing on me?"

She laughed. "The others wanted to know why they were here, or who I was. You ask me what the purpose of the testing is. How delightful. The purpose of the testing is to see if you are useful to us. That tells you no more than you knew before. But it does display a certain creativity. The other questions would have told you no more than you knew before. You should prove interesting."

With that, she turned and walked out, humming a Haydn concerto.

One question, and I had blown it. Or had I? Now I knew that there had been other men or perhaps women who had been subjected to her "testing," Her manner and treatment of me
reminded me of...what? I thought about it. A zookeeper? A psychologist? Zira from the movie *Planet of the Apes*. Right. *Take your filthy hands off of me you damned dirty ape.*

What was the name of the tune she was humming?

I shivered. I had to escape this place. Wherever or whatever it was.

She returned, dressed in a gray uniform and short boots. In her hand was a leash and collar. Dangling from her belt were a set of leg irons and a short riding crop. She bent over and unlocked the door to the pen. "Crawl out. Do not stand until told. Do not speak. Do you understand these orders?"

I nodded. I had to play along and gain her confidence. As soon as she dropped her guard, I would attack and escape.

I crawled out and waited. As she approached to place the collar on me, I tried to spring on her. My attempt was blocked by her booted foot kicking me in the side, rolling me onto my back.

Her voice was cold and smoking, like dry ice. "You respond to my kindness by attacking me. You are in error; you will be corrected."

With that she placed her boot on my cock and balls and placed her weight on them.
The pressure increased until I wanted to scream. I wasn't going to give her that satisfaction.

Great intentions. Bad performance. I started whimpering as the pressure became more intense. I lay gasping in pain. The pressure stopped. The leg irons were clamped onto me and the leash was used to tie my hands to the collar she placed around my neck.

"Stand up, M-5. There are tests to be run, and you have delayed us long enough."

I lay on the floor helpless to resist physically. "That is not my name. I am Michael...," I started to say and was cut off by the crop slashing across my thighs.

"You have no name. You are subject M-5. Nothing more, and potentially less, if you continue to resist. Is that clear to you, M-5?"

I said nothing. I didn't even nod. I waited.

"Excellent. You may speak."

"I understand."

The crop slashed across me again. She prompted, "I understand... what?"

"I understand...Mistress."

Another slash.

"The proper form of address is 'I understand, Controller.'"

"I understand, Controller," I corrected.

"Good, M-5. M-1 through M-4 were not entirely successful. I

expect that you will be of more use than they were. Now, stand up. Do not speak. Nod, if you understand the orders."

I nodded quickly and got to my feet as directed. The leg irons made walking difficult. I was ordered back into the room with the table. This time my collar was attached to a chain hanging from a ring in the ceiling. The leg irons were locked to another ring in the floor, spreading my legs.

"This test is simple, M-5. I am going to attach weights to your balls to see how much weight you can tolerate. I will then repeat the process with your nipples."

A leather strap with a hook was clamped around my balls. The Controller removed a set of weights from a cabinet and showed them to me. "Each weight is one ounce. I have sixty-four weights here. Perhaps you will be more successful than M-2. He could not hold more than thirty-two before he…failed the test."

She attached the first weight to the hook. It pulled the strap tighter. She attached the next, and then another. With each, the pain increased. Four, five, six weights. Then, a seventh and eighth weight.

She paused. "You are doing well, M-5. Are you in pain? You may speak."

"Yes, Controller."

"Only fifty-six more to go, M-5. Can you do it?"

"I don't know, Controller," I moaned.

"We will both find out, M-5."

Another weight, and then another. Ten, eleven, twelve.

I cried out in pain. I felt a coldness touch my balls. There was a thud.

Then, the pain stopped.

A gentle hand touched my face and stroked my aching balls.

I opened my eyes to see the Controller holding a knife and smiling. "M-2 failed the test, because he did not admit to his pain. You did. If you do not confess your pain, you are of no use to us. I believe the nipple tests are unnecessary. Are you willing to be whipped as a replacement test? You may speak."

"Yes, Controller. Thank you," I whispered.

"For what, M-5?" she asked, amused.

"For giving me a choice, Controller."

"You have shown you are intelligent enough to make a choice. Prepare yourself." With that she turned and walked towards a rack of whips on the other side of the room.

She returned with three whips, one with wide straps, one with knots in the ends, and one with thin tails. "I will use these on you. You will tell me which one I have used by saying the Number One, Two or Three."

She held up the wide one. "Number One."

Then, the thin one. "Number Two."

Lastly, the knotted one. "Number Three."

As she walked behind me, she continued to speak. "If you make an error in identifying the whips, I shall start over from the beginning. You will endure ten strokes from each. If you are correct with your answers, you will have taken thirty strokes. If not, the number could be much higher. We begin."

The first one felt like a bee sting across my ass.

"Two," I said.

The next one thudded across my back.

"One," I moaned.

The next fell across my shoulders.

"Three."

The strokes increased and changed focus. Faster and harder they came. I chanted what I thought were the correct numbers. I soon lost count of the number of strokes.

My world dissolved into the feel of the whips and my own labored chanting.

After an unknown amount of time, she stopped and stood before me. "You are progressing well. I will release your hands."

I collapsed at her booted feet like a puppet whose strings had been cut.

"Kiss my boots, M-5. Show your appreciation for the attention I have given you," she commanded.

I licked the slick leather of her boots and tried to organize my whirling thoughts. The pain was becoming a drug. A strange, wonderful, terrible drug. And she became more pleased as I endured more abuse. And as the abuse increased, my desire to give her pleasure increased as well.

Why? I was being hurt. But, she wanted me to suffer for her. She desired my pain. This was madness. But, she stroked and comforted me when the pain became too much to bear. She fed and watered me. She cleaned me. She punished me and cared for me.

I felt something in myself stir. I had always cared for others and seldom thought of my needs and desires.

She cared about me in her own way.

I drifted into sleep with my face pressed into her boots.

III

I awoke crying out in the darkness. I was still chained to the ring in the floor.

Her voice came from the velvet darkness. "Why do you cry out, M-5?"

I paused, uncertain of speaking.

"You may speak. What frightens you in the darkness?"

"I thought I was alone. I'm sorry I spoke without permission, Controller."

"You lost someone you loved, didn't you?" she whispered.

I howled. "How could you know that?"

"I know. I know your mind and your soul. You endure the pain, because you know pain.
Your soul is far from peace, and your spirit is in torment. I know your pain. When the time comes, you will offer it to me. But, you still have much to prove."

A light flickered in the darkness. She approached me, illuminated by a single candle. She was wearing a sheer black robe. She gazed down at me with pity in her eyes. After a moment, she turned away. "I will never leave you…"

The candle went out, and I was again in darkness.

Time passed. And as time passed, so did the fear.

How strange that I should trust someone who had given me so much pain.

Through a high window I could see the darkness give way to the gray of dawn.

I suppose I had fallen asleep when I was again awakened by a warm stream of water. I looked up to see her standing over me, holding her robe aside, pissing on my helpless body.

She stopped when she saw me watching.

"Open your mouth, M-5. I have a gift for you."

I hesitated, perhaps too long to suit her.

A cold gleam came into her eyes. "You refuse to obey me?"

I opened my mouth, closed my eyes, and waited for the acrid stream.

It never came.

Instead, I tasted apple juice, sweet and warm.

"You see, M-5, obedience can be rewarding. Oh, someday you will beg for my hot wine, but not now. You must earn that privilege."

She walked out of the room and returned in a few moments in a red body suit and carrying a hood. She quickly placed the hood over my head and secured it to my collar with a small lock. Unlocking the floor chain, she ordered me to my feet.

When the hood was removed, I was in a proper bathroom with a shower and toilet. On the counter appeared a tray of food and an hourglass.

After removing my restraints, she turned the glass over. "Eat and wash yourself. I shall return for you when the sand runs out."

The door closed, and I heard a bolt slide and lock. I ate quickly and got into the shower. There was no soap, but the hot water was plentiful. When I got out of the shower, I looked in the mirror over the sink. Even allowing for the distortion caused by the unbreakable glass of the mirror, I looked a sight. I had a growth of beard at least a week old. How long had I been a captive? The hourglass was my first actual time indicator. I sat and watched it, trying to regain my sense of time.

She returned with the hood, leash and collar. This time she was dressed in a red dress; her hair was pulled back into a tight bun. On her hip hung a long whip.

"You will follow all of my orders. Any disobedience will be punished. Up to now, you have only been corrected. Punishment is much more severe. Do you understand, M-5? Nod, if you do."

I nodded and knelt before her.

"I see that you do understand, M-5. I am pleased."

I was fitted with the hood and collar and led out of the room. A few moments later, she instructed me to climb a short flight of steps and stop five paces from the top.

I did as I was told.

"This is subject M-5. The subject's test results are displayed for your approval. I will demonstrate his pain tolerance now."

The first lash startled me, and I had to bite the inside of the hood to keep from making any sound. The strokes continued until my knees started to buckle.

"M-5, resume your position," she commanded.

I struggled upright again and stood swaying, waiting for the strokes to begin.

"As you can see, the subject has a high tolerance. This demonstration was five points over his tested rating. His ability to obey is Good to Excellent. I recommend this subject for advanced training."

There was a pause that seemed like an eternity.

"Subject M-5 is to receive advanced training starting now," she announced.

IV

Advanced training. What was that? I was led back to the pen where I had spent my first night and ordered to kneel while the hood was removed. Two changes had been made. There was now a small pillow in the cage, and an embossed metal sign was mounted on the door. *M-5*.

"This will be your home for the duration of your training. If you perform well, you will be rewarded. Mistakes will be corrected; disobedience will be punished. Do you understand the difference between punishment and correction, M-5?"

I knelt mute before her. I was unsure as to if I should nod, reply or bark.

"Do you understand the difference between the two, M-5? Speak up!"

"I think I do, Controller," I responded softly.

"I will give you an example. If you speak to me without my permission, you will be corrected. If you commit any act of overt disobedience, you will be punished. Correction is unpleasant. Punishment is…well, I'll leave you to wonder. Just remember I know what is painful for you and how far I can take you without lasting physical damage. Of course your mental state…"

I did not like the idea of what she was saying. And she knew it.

"You have a question for me, M-5? You may speak," she prompted.

"How long will--" I started to ask.

"Will you be here?" she finished. "As long as it takes to train you to serve us properly. You will be trained to serve us in any way that might be desirable to us. And when you are trained, you will no longer wish to leave."

She laughed softly at the expression on my face. "The idea frightens you. How amusing. You fear being possessed, but you also fear being abandoned."

I did not know how to respond.

Stroking my head like a pet dog, she continued, "The other fears you have, even the unspoken ones, will bind you to us."

She opened the pen door and directed me inside. "You will rest now. When next you and I meet, you will discover who we are."

She left me locked in the pen, to wait. Was she right? Was it my fears that would enslave me to her?

When she returned, she was dressed in a black sheath dress and carried a silver-handled cane. "Do I need to use the leash or binders on you, M-5? Or, can you be trusted to obey without question? Your failure to obey would embarrass me greatly and result in a great deal of pain for you."

"I will obey you, Controller." I wasn't sure if it were the promised pain, or the fact I might cause her embarrassment that prompted my reply. For some reason, I wanted her to take pride in me.

"Very well. I am going to take you to see the others in our group. You will not speak to them unless I order it. You will not speak to me other than to answer 'yes' or 'no' to any direct question I may ask. You will answer only 'yes' or 'no', and you will be truthful in your answers.
No matter what the question, you will answer it. If I find you were not truthful later, I will punish you, and if you have lied to anyone else, they will punish you. Is that well understood?"

"Yes, Controller."

She unlocked the pen and ordered me to exit and to stand up. She led me down a hallway and to a large carved oak door. Above the door was an inscription. It said one word: Ay'esha.

Ay'esha. My mind churned. Then, I remembered. An old novel by H. Rider Haggard. Ay'esha meant: *She who must be obeyed.*

My Controller watched me read the inscription. She smiled in delight for the first time.

"You are aware of the meaning of the word, I see. Now you understand who we are." She opened the door and led me through it.

I was now in a well-furnished room, and facing me were two women. Untold, I looked down at the floor. One was older than my controller and the other seemed to be the same age. They were both dressed elegantly, and I felt out of place in my nakedness and beard.

My Controller sat in a high-backed chair and ordered me onto my hands and knees next to her, with my head up. After a moment, I felt a weight set upon my back.

"Do not move, M-5, or you may be injured."

I froze into position. I could feel warmth on my back where the weight was centered.
This continued until she sighed and said, "That was a lovely cup of tea."

The weight was removed and the spot on my back slowly cooled.

She chatted for a time with the other women about a variety of things, ignoring me.

"He seems to make a very nice table," the older woman said. "Has he ever done it before, do you know?"

"Let's find out, shall we? M-5, have you ever been a table?" the Controller asked.

"No."

"Have you ever been used as any type of furniture before now?"

"No."

"Have you ever been used as a sex toy before?"

I hesitated. And, blushed.

The delay was rewarded by a stroke of the cane across my ass.

"Answer me, M-5."

"No."

"Have you ever thought of being used as a sex toy?" questioned the older woman.

I didn't answer. It couldn't be answered as 'yes' or 'no'. I had thoughts of being used sexually, fantasies, and dreams. But converting them to reality?

After a few seconds, my Controller dismissed the question as foolish and turned the conversation away from me and back to other subjects.

The younger of the two women was not willing to dismiss the question so easily. "M-5, this is a direct question. Have you ever thought of being used as a sex toy? Answer me!"

I stayed mute. I had been told not to respond. I would not respond.

After a minute of waiting, the woman stood and approached me. She wore a coiled whip at her belt and began uncoiling it as she approached. "I think he's being insolent, Minx. I want an answer to my question. And I'll have one, even if I have to beat it out of him!"

I held my position. I was scared. She was angry. Was my Controller going to protect me? What if she didn't? I must not panic. Do not show fear.

"Lydia," said the older woman. "He may have a reason for not answering. What if he is following the orders of his Controller?"

Minx, my Controller, laughed.

"You always did know me, Anna. You are wise indeed to have suspected that." Turning to the one named Lydia, she added, "He has been instructed not to speak to anyone without a direct order from me."

"So order him to answer," Lydia insisted.

"Are you questioning my judgment, Lydia?" she hissed. "I alone will control him, I alone will give his orders, and I will protect him from you, you who would punish rather than correct. You, who would destroy him rather than build him? No, he is mine to do with as I will."

Lydia turned away. I could see the hate in her eyes. Hate for me, for everything that my Controller was saying.

"I believe you should remove him from this room, Minx," instructed Anna. "It seems that he is a disruptive force."

"As you wish, Anna. But, he was carrying out my orders. If there was a disruption, I am responsible for it."

With that my Controller ordered me to my feet, and out of the room ahead of her.

As soon as the door shut, I was on my knees in front of her shaking and weeping.

"What is wrong little one? Tell me!"

"I caused a problem for you, Controller. I'm sorry I failed you," I wept.

"You did not fail me. You obeyed your orders exactly as I gave them to you. The question was no business of Lydia's. And, I already know the answer from you anyway."

"You do?" I said through the tears.

"Of course, I do. You wish to be considered desirable; all men do. The idea of becoming a sex toy is an appealing one to some people. But consider that a sex toy is used and then put away. There is no consideration for a sex toy's feelings. A sex toy exists to serve. You exist to serve our needs. Those needs cover far more and far less than sex, for our purposes. You will be a sex toy at some point, but not something to be used and thrown away."

I needed to process what she was telling me.

"Now come along. It is time for your feeding."

V

My physical training started that very evening. My Controller, dressed in a white lab coat, led me back to the room with the table.

I saw for the first time it was equipped as a medical examination room.

She placed me on a scale, adjusted it and frowned in displeasure. "You are overweight, M-5. The change in your diet will remove a certain amount, but not enough to suit me. You will be exercised twice a day until I am satisfied."

She continued her examination with the same care as lavished on a side of beef being inspected. And actually, both were for the same purpose.

The results of the blood pressure check also annoyed her. "Your blood pressure is higher than it should be. Obviously, exercise was not on your list of priorities."

"Controller," I ventured. "Perhaps my blood pressure is higher in response to you."

"Perhaps, it is." She slapped me across the face. "You were not given permission to speak. And if I want your opinion, I will ask for it. Is that very clear?"

I nodded, feeling the sting on my cheek.

"Good. You do understand. Now, stand there quietly while I finish checking you."

I stood and waited while she checked my eyes and ears, then the fabled, "Open your mouth and say 'Ahhh'."

She finished taking notes and walked to a cabinet. When she turned back, she was carrying a syringe.

My knees started to buckle, and I trembled.

"I see that I have found one of your fears, M-5. You fear needles. Interesting. However, I will now take a blood sample from you. I will bind you to the table, if you do not cooperate willingly. I will give you one chance only."

I stood still, except for my shaking, as she approached. The fear grew, and only the fear of being punished kept me in place.

In one swift motion she tied the arm and slipped the needle into a vein. As she withdrew the needle, I collapsed on the floor.

She placed the sample on a counter and returned to my side. She stroked my head and held me until the shaking stopped. She wiped away my hot tears and told me that she would help me with my fears.

After a few moments, she helped me to my feet and led me to a treadmill. Attached to the side rails of the treadmill were a set of restraints on a short chain. Next to the head of the treadmill were a medical monitor and a set of medical sensors.

She ordered me onto the treadmill and attached the restraints. Working quickly, she attached the sensors to my arms, legs and torso. "Now, you will start out walking. After a short time, the treadmill will speed up. Ultimately, you will find yourself running. If you slow your pace, I have ways to speed you up. Each day the running time will increase, and the walking time will decrease. The sensors will record your performance."

Before I could react, she had set the machine in motion. At the beginning it wasn't too bad, but as the speed increased, it became more and more tiring. I slowed my pace once and was rewarded by a slash across my ass with a buggy whip that I had not noticed her taking out. The torture continued for what felt like an hour, but couldn't have been that long.

Suddenly, the treadmill slowed to a stop. I stood panting and sweating, heart pounding wildly.

"A good start, M-5. Tomorrow morning, we will work a bit longer." She freed me from the restraints and tangle of sensor wires and walked me to the bathroom and shower, locking me in again.

She returned after a few minutes and was waiting for me when I exited the shower. She toweled me dry and started rubbing an ointment into my aching legs. After a few minutes, she stood up and pronounced me fit.

"I do not wish you to stiffen during the night in your pen. The ointment will prevent that from happening."

I wanted to thank her, but I remembered the slap.

She smiled. "You have already thanked me, M-5. I can see it in your eyes. You must be properly taken care of. Any injury would reduce your ability to serve us."

With that, she returned me to my pen and covered it for the night.

When we began again in the morning, she attached the restraints and sensors and started the treadmill again. "I shall return in a few minutes with your morning ration."

She left me to the tender mercies of the machine. I kept up the pace, and then got tired. I decided to slow down.

ZAP! An electric shock ran up my leg. It threw me off balance. I staggered and felt another shock.

I picked up the pace, and the shocks stopped.

The treadmill increased its speed. Another shock, as I slowed. Faster it moved and faster and faster the shocks came as I failed to keep up.

The shocks stopped as the treadmill slowed to a halt.

I stood panting as my Controller returned to the room with a tray of food, a full tray of food. Bacon, eggs, toast, juice, even coffee.

She looked at me and then looked at the strip of paper that had recorded the session.

"I told you that I had ways of encouraging you to perform. You have just found one of the more unforgettable ways. There are also more enjoyable ones you may discover in time. You disobeyed and were corrected. You have, however, forfeited your meal for this morning. You may, however, watch me eat."

Releasing me from my bonds, she ordered me to sit at her feet and watch her eat. She took her time, savoring every bite of it. At one point she toyed with a piece of bacon and teased me with it, waving it under my nose. Then, with great deliberation, ate it. She patted her lips with the napkin and sighed in satisfaction.

"Perhaps, you will do better this afternoon. You may lick the plate clean."

And, I did.

VI

After my meal of crumbs and grease, she re-collared me and chained me to the floor ring. She left the room and returned a few minutes later with a leash, some items of fur and a mask. A dog mask.

"Now, M-5, we will find out if you are at least as intelligent as a dog. Of course, you need to look the part, so I have some items to help." She placed the mask on my face, and attached some fur booties to my hands and feet. "Now, for the final touch. Dogs have tails, and you don't have one...yet."

The last fur item was a tail. And at the root of the tail, it had a piece of plastic, rounded, and about two inches in diameter.

I started to cringe away from her. Her response was to slap me across the ass.

"Bad dog! I guess I have to teach you to heel."

She lubricated the plastic tail fitting and started towards me. I dropped from all fours to flat on the floor. She placed the tail on the floor and started pulling on my leash to get me up. I went limp and offered no resistance. I also offered no help.

"Well, I see we have a little problem here, M-5. Are you disobeying an order from me?"

I said nothing. I guess I was actually being disobedient. But, I really didn't want that shoved in my ass.

"Now, what would be the best way to punish you and still get what I want?" she mused.

Then, she knelt next to me and started tickling my ribs. I tried not to react, but couldn't help it. I started wiggling and thrashing. As soon as my back arched up, she slapped my legs apart, and with a swift motion, slid the tail piece into my ass. She continued to tickle me until I begged for her to stop.

"Why should I stop punishing you, M-5? You disobeyed me. Tell me why I should stop."

"Please, Controller, it hurts so much. I'm sorry, please stop," I begged.

"What hurts, M-5? The tail or the tickling? Tell me," she demanded.

"The tickling hurts me, Controller."

"Then, you will wear the tail piece until I remove it, if I stop tickling you?" she suggested.

By then, I was in tearful agony. I would do anything for her at this point, if she would only stop. "Yes, Controller, please. I promise."

She stopped tickling me and stood up. "Bark for me, M-5. I want to hear what kind of dog you sound like."

I barked.

"Higher, M-5. I want to hear a small dog."

I yipped in soprano, and she laughed.

"I don't think so. Try lower. You are not a lap dog."

I barked in basso profundo.

"Much better. You will bark like that on command or when you need to attract my attention. Understood?"

I barked again.

"Much better, M-5. Now let's go for our walkies." She unlocked the chain and led me on all fours out of the room. She led me down the hall back to my pen, then towards the main meeting room.

We passed the young woman named Lydia on the way down the hallway.

"I see you have him under better control this time, Minx. And what a fine dog he makes.
Of course, he'd be even better, if you had him fixed. If fact, if you like, I could do that for you."

My Controller laughed at that idea. "Lydia, you amaze me. He hasn't even been bred yet, and you want to deprive him of siring a litter of puppies. We need to maintain the gene pool, you know."

"Drain it, you mean. Really, Minx, what are they good for?"

"If you haven't discovered their multiple uses by now, Lydia, you never will. Good day."

She tugged on my lead, and we continued our walkies.

As I shambled along as a poorly equipped dog, I wondered what had prompted such hatred in Lydia for the male of the species. Actually, I didn't know how she felt about women, so it could have been life in general she hated.

I stayed close to my Controller as we walked. I felt that the discussion with Lydia had upset her. I barked for her attention.

"What is it, M-5?"

I turned back towards where we had passed Lydia and whimpered.

"Did she frighten you, M-5?"

I barked twice.

"Then, what is it, M-5?"

I whimpered at her and turned towards the spot again.

"Did she upset me? Is that it?"

I barked once.

"No, M-5, she didn't upset me. She is who she is, as I am who I am."

I nuzzled her leg.

"Yes, M-5, I know. Her hatred frightens me at time, too. But, I will protect you." She led me back to the room where my pen was and removed the leash. "Now, let's see if you know any tricks that would amuse me. Sit!"

I got up on my knees and held my position. The tail probed deeper into me.

"Roll over!"

I dropped to my side and did a roll.

"Play dead!"

I rolled onto my back and stiffened up. I held my position as she walked towards me. I was totally exposed and the tail was painfully compressed under me.

She reached down and scratched my belly. How did dogs react?

I started thrashing one leg. She moved lower and started scratching my balls. I started becoming erect.

"Good dog!" she laughed, as I flailed my leg faster in response to her touch. "Horny puppy dog. That pleases me."

She took her hand away, and I stopped moving my leg.

"Perhaps we need to find a bitch for you to fuck. Would you like that, M-5? A nice hot bitch to put your seed into? That might be amusing to watch."

My erection got harder.

"You are a little pervert, aren't you? Thinking about fucking a bitch. Perhaps being fucked yourself?"

My erection started collapsing.

"That doesn't interest you? Well, perhaps you won't be given a choice. If I want to take your sorry ass and give it to a bitch or a stud, I will. I control what you do and who or what you do it with. Remember that. You are here to give pleasure at my whim. And, I will train you to give it in all ways. Even if you do not enjoy them, you will give pleasure to others."

She reattached the leash and ordered me onto all fours again. I rolled onto my hands and knees. My tail bobbed with the motion. I started becoming unaware of it; it started being a natural part of me. But my bladder was getting to be a problem. I whimpered and pulled at the lead.

"Do you have a problem, M-5?"

I whimpered again and strained towards a corner of the room.

"Do you need to pee, M-5?"

I barked an affirmative.

"Sit. Stay! I will be back." She dropped the lead and left the room. She returned with a small tree in a pot. "Now, M-5, you may pee on the tree like a good dog."

I started to rise, and she yanked my lead.

"Lift your leg on it like a real dog. And you'd better not make a mess, or you'll clean it up...with your tongue."

I moved to the tree and raised a leg. I will tell you now; I don't understand how dogs aim for anything, let alone a tree. I did the best I could, but some of it dribbled onto the floor.

She dragged me around and forced my face into the wetness. My beard started soaking up the urine puddle.

"Now lick your lips. I want you to taste yourself!"

She said it so fiercely, I did it without thinking. It was bitter and salty.

"Good dog. Now back in your pen, and I'll feed you." She led me back to the pen and unhooked the lead. I crawled inside and started sucking at the water bottle to remove the taste from my mouth.

"You will learn to enjoy it, M-5. In fact, you will beg to taste mine."

VII

My meal was beef chunks in gravy. It looked like dog food, but tasted ambrosial after missing a meal. Eating with the dog mask on was a challenge. In fact I started thinking my beard caught more food than my mouth.

All during my meal my Controller watched me eat. I wondered what she was thinking about.

I soon found out. After I finished with my meal, she removed the food pan, placed it on a counter and then unlocked my pen.

"Crawl out, M-5," she instructed.

I crawled out and waited as she removed the fake dog paws from my hands and feet. She removed the mask and then walked behind me to study my tail.

"Perhaps I should leave it in you to remind you of your place as a dog, but I think the collar will do for now."

She removed the tail from my aching asshole and placed it on the counter as well.

Reattaching the lead, she ordered me to follow, only this time on my feet instead of as a dog.

She led me back to the examining room and ordered me to lay face up on the table. I knew better than to fail to comply with her orders in this matter. I lay down, and she strapped my arms and legs, so I could not move them.

After strapping me in, she walked out of my vision and then returned holding a can of shaving cream, a basin of water and a razor. A straight edge razor that glinted in the light. I cringed.

"Now, M-5, I did notice your beard was becoming a bit of a problem, so I am going to shave you. After all, you need to stay neat. I shave, too. Perhaps you noticed that. Perhaps not.
Lie still, and you won't be hurt."

She proceeded to lather my face.

"Let's see how still you can lie. I haven't shaved a man's pubic area in a long time, and I might cut you if you move too much."

She started on my face. Quickly she removed the growth of beard and then started on my chest.

"Not much hair there. I'll try not to cut off a nipple by accident."

I held even more still after that comment.

She progressed lower. Almost lovingly, she applied shaving cream to my pubic area and slowly held the razor over my balls. As she started to shave them, her handling of them started my erection again.

"Be very careful not to get too aroused, or I might do as Lydia suggested by accident."

The razor moved out of my line of sight, and I felt the blade skimming across my skin. Back and forth the blade went until she raised it into my line of sight, and it was covered with hair and cream. She wiped it and then took a hold of my cock. Skillfully, she ran the blade down my cock, peeling away the hair matting the base of it. I felt a slight pull and heard her mutter.

"Almost had an accident, M-5. I wouldn't want to remove a mole, you know."

I was both aroused and in fear. The blade could slip, and I would be singing soprano.

She concentrated on her work and soon put the razor down and wiped away the cream with a damp towel. "Now you look like a little boy again. A hairless, little boy."

She stroked my still erect cock. "Such an interesting piece of meat. It enlarges or contracts. It shows emotional states, and it makes such a divine torture device. A man will do almost anything to have it touched. But, the touch can be torture, as well. Can't it, M-5? You want me to make you shoot your seed, and I have no interest in doing that at all."

I didn't know how to respond.

"I just like to tease them and make my toys beg. I like using their desires to drive them into submission to my will. As you are becoming more aroused, you are becoming more receptive to my orders. You would do anything I order you to do, if I were to give you release."

I moaned as she teased the tip of my cock with her fingernails. She was right. I would do anything for release at that point. I hated it. I hated being controlled by my lust. I was not an animal. But I had been made one, reduced to thinking with my glands.

"Yes, you are an animal now, M-5. If I were to free your restraints, you would seize me and rape me. This is what you are inside. An animal maddened by lust. You will learn to control it again, M-5. You will be trained to unleash it when we desire."

With that she poured ice water on my erect cock and watched it collapse as I screamed in shock.

She left me there tied and helpless for a long time. I could see the daylight fade into darkness through the window set high in the wall.

When she returned, she was dressed in a red silk sheath dress with a slit up one side. Accompanying her was a young Asian girl dressed in a red kimono and carrying a small box.

"Are you awake, M-5? You may speak."

"Yes, Controller, I am awake."

"Good. M-5, this is Mei Ling. She is going to help you with your fears. She is very good at what she does, M-5, and you will refer to her as Master, if she chooses to speak to you. Is that understood?"

"Yes, Controller. She is to be referred to as Master."

"Very good. Mei Ling, please show M-5 what you have in the box," she said, turning to the other woman.

"Yes, Controller Minx, I would be pleased to do so." She opened the box and displayed the contents.

Needles. Needles of all lengths and sizes.

"Please, Controller, no," I begged.

"Why not, M-5? What will you do to avoid the needles? Tell me."

I couldn't think. The sight of the needles had caused my mind to go blank.

My Controller laughed. "He wants to avoid the needles, Mei Ling, but can't think of any way to do it. Perhaps we should insert a few and see if that starts him thinking."

"The use of the needles in special places does stimulate brain function, Controller Minx. Perhaps I should start?"

"Not just yet. Perhaps I should give him some suggestions. M-5, would you kiss my feet to avoid the needles?"

"Yes, Controller."

"Would you kiss my ass to avoid the needles?"

"Yes!"

"Would you kiss Lydia's ass to avoid the needles?"

I paused. "Yes."

"Willingly?"

"No, Controller. But, I would do it."

"Good boy. You are being truthful. You will serve Lydia some time, and you will do so willingly. But, I will not force it upon you now. You will now face the needles, if you do not give me a reason to stop."

Perhaps now was the time she had warned me about. "I will drink your piss, Controller."

She laughed. "My piss is a sacrament, not a punishment, M-5. I should punish you for that error, but you are a dumb animal after all, so I will overlook it. Mei Ling, you may prepare the needles."

My Controller stepped to the head of the table and strapped my head down. I could no longer see the Master and the needles. But, I knew she was there, and the fear grew in me. My Controller had promised to help. Had she decided to change her mind? I closed my eyes and waited.

I felt a pressure on my body, and then my Controller ordered me to open my eyes. I opened them to see my Controller squatting over my face. She had the most perfect ass and pussy I had ever seen.

"I thought you might enjoy being gagged in this way, smothered under my ass rather than a hard rubber ball. Do you like that idea better, M-5?"

"Oh, yes, Controller. Thank you, Controller."

"When we are through, you will thank the Master in any way

that might please her. You will thank her for giving you pain or pleasure, whatever she demands or desires."

"Yes, Controller."

She settled her ass on my face. I could still breathe, but not deeply. Her smell entranced me. Her woman musk and the smell of her ass. It had been too long since I smelled the scent of a woman.

"You may begin, Mei Ling."

I waited for the stab of pain. It never came. I felt a burst of warmth in my leg, then nothing. The same in my arm. My chest. Each time a burst of warmth, and then nothing. Or, something. I begin to feel very relaxed again, almost floating. I soon no longer cared. My world was one of woman's scent and warmth. My mind became fuzzy.

After an unknown amount of time, my Controller got off me and stood next to my head.

"Do you hear me, M-5?" she asked gently.

Her voice sounded a million miles away. I whispered, "Yes, Controller."

"Do you feel pain, M-5?"

"No, Controller."

She picked up a mirror and held it so I could see my body.

I was a human pincushion! Needles were inserted all over my body. But, there was no pain, no blood. Just warmth.

"How..."

"The Master is a master of acupuncture. She inserted the needles into the places on your body that can make you feel pleasure. Needles can not harm you; ignorance can. Your mind controls your body, M-5. Soon you will be able to block out pain and find only pleasure in it."

She ordered the Master to begin withdrawing the needles. As she did, the warmth decreased, but the pain never came.

When she was done she joined my Controller at the head of the table. "Do you have anything to say to me, M-5?"

"Thank you, Master. Thank you for giving me pleasure."

She reached out and touched my face gently. "I remove pain and fear from those who truly need it removed. But, the pain in your soul can not be touched by my talents. Offer it to the Goddess of All."

"I am in your debt, Mei Ling." My Controller asked, "How shall

I repay you for this service?"

"You own me nothing. But, I charge him with the debt. He shall serve you long and well."

"And for you personally, Mei Ling? What shall I give you?"

I saw the Master smile and reach out to stroke the face of my Controller. "I desire your lovemaking ,Controller Minx. Nothing more than that."

"And you shall have it. But, what of M-5? Should I return him to his pen for the night?"

There was a long thoughtful silence. "No, bring him, gagged and tethered. He should see what passions his pain stirs in us."

VIII

I was hooded and gagged before being released from the table. Releasing the bonds from the table, they quickly used a rope to tie my hands behind my back. I heard the snap of the leash and was led off.

I was pushed into something soft and rolled over. The hood was stripped off, and I saw I was in a bedroom. The lighting was subdued, and there was the scent of incense in the air. The bed was wide and looked soft. The sheets looked like silk the way they glimmered in the light.

My Controller and the Master looked at me, and they both smiled.

"Now, my little toy, see what your pain has brought us?" said my Controller.

She removed her dress as the Master dropped her kimono to the floor. I noticed for the first time that my Controller's nipples were pierced. The Master had a tattoo of a dragon across her upper arm.

They embraced and kissed passionately. They stroked each other gently. I could see my Controller's nipples erect as the Master nibbled at them. She pulled at them with her teeth, stretching them. My Controller shivered in pleasure. The Controller bit the Master's nipples. She writhed.

"Now, M-5, watch us. Do not turn away."

They lay down on the bed together. She placed her hand between the Master's thighs and grabbed her pussy. There was a soft moan that the Controller smothered with a kiss. They continued stroking and touching.

I could smell the musk of these two women as they made passionate love. I could no longer think of them as Master and Controller. They became Minx and Mei Ling, to be cherished, to be watched in their joy and pleasure. Had I really been the catalyst for this? I found myself becoming aroused, more that I had been in many years. I wanted to join them in their joy. I read once that shared pain is lessened and shared joy is increased. I felt honored to witness their love making.

I moaned into my gag as Minx buried her face in Mei Ling's wetness. She turned so that Mei Ling could pleasure her with her mouth, as well. The moaning and breathing became more rapid. There was a pause, and then I could see them both orgasm. Watching them was like staring into the heart of an exploding star. Their joy and beauty was blinding and pure as the first light of creation. I wept. I had not felt such love between two people since - - I blotted out the thought. That time was in my past, not to be recaptured.

This was a sharing of life, a celebration.

They broke from their embrace and looked towards me. As I watched their faces I saw in them a love I had not seen in years, and they saw the tears of joy in my eyes.

"You see, M-5, the love you lost does still exist. It has not gone from this world," Minx said gently.

"Listen to her, M-5. In time and with our help, it will find you again," Mei Ling, the Master, advised.

"Would you like some small part of our joy, M-5?" Minx asked kindly.

I nodded. She rolled off the bed and looked at Mei Ling. Mei Ling nodded. The gag was removed and Minx reached between Mei Ling's legs and stroked her wetness. She took her gleaming fingers and placed them in my mouth. I sucked on them greedily. I savored the taste of her like a fine wine. Mei Ling stroked her fingers between Minx's legs and offered them to me. They tasted sweet, where her juices had tasted spicy.

They took me from the chair and attached my lead to the foot of the bed.

"You will sleep at our feet tonight, M-5. And tomorrow, you will serve us both."

With that, Mei Ling turned out the light, and I was left in warm darkness, with the sweet and spicy tastes of these two women on my lips, and the image of their lovemaking in my mind.

I was awakened the next morning by a soft kiss on the forehead. I opened my eyes to see Minx smiling at me. "Good morning, M-5. The Master is still sleeping, so speak quietly. Did you enjoy yourself last night?"

"Yes, Controller, I did," I whispered.

"Mei Ling was pleased with your reaction, as was I. You watched as instructed and did not distract us. And yes, I did see how aroused you were. Would you like to see more?"

I blushed at that. "I'm sorry, Controller."

"I didn't ask if you were sorry. I asked if you would like to see more," she hissed.

"Oh, yes, Controller," I whispered in response.

"You will have to pay for it with your pain again. Do you understand?"

I thought about it. Was the pain I knew she could inflict worth it? Was the joy I witnessed worth it? "Yes, Controller. I understand."

"Why do you wish to suffer the pain, M-5?"

"Because it gives you pleasure."

"Does pain give you pleasure, M-5?" she pressed quietly.

"No, Controller. But --" It struck me suddenly. I didn't like pain, but I wanted to please her.

"But, what, M-5? Tell me."

"I just want to please you, Controller."

"I will accept that for now. But, you will give me a proper reason soon."

IX

Mei Ling woke up at that point stretched and sat up. She kissed Minx softly before addressing me.

"Good morning, M-5. I trust you slept well?"

"Very well, Master. May I inquire as to your rest?"

"I slept well. You pleased me greatly with your behavior. You will be rewarded."

"Thank you, Master, but I wish no reward for following instructions. I was following orders."

"I understand that, but you followed them very well." She turned back to Minx. "How long have you had him in your pens Minx?"

"I have only had him for…well, less time that you might think. He seems to have a natural talent, a bit unrefined, but there is potential," Minx replied.

"M-5, can you cook?"

"Yes, Master, I can cook."

"Good. Go through the door at the far end of the room. You will find a small kitchen. You will fix us some breakfast and bring it to us. Show me how creative you can be. Go."

I started to get up, but was pulled back down by the lead attached to the bed.

"Well, I will say he follows orders well, Minx," she laughed. "Perhaps you should release him."

Minx released the lead, and untied me. "Go."

I went through the indicated door and found a small, well stocked kitchen. I also found something I had not seen in awhile. A window. It looked out onto a courtyard with a fountain, splashing quietly. I could see the sky for the first time in days. And flowers, beautiful red flowers.

There was also a door. Escape! I started towards the door and then stopped. Where was I going to go? I was naked, no money, no real idea where I was.

And, then I thought about it. Did I really want to escape? I was being treated like an animal; I was being tortured and abused. And, I was being cared for, even...loved.

A dog's life. And, really, what's wrong with a dog's life? They're fed, cared for, and all they give in return is devotion and service.

I turned away from the door and started fixing breakfast, refreshed by the view of life in the outside world. Breakfast wasn't fancy, just scrambled eggs, bacon, toast, and coffee. I placed them on a tray and reentered the bedroom.

Both of the women were gone. I placed the tray onto a table and kneeled next to it to wait. After a short time, both Minx and Mei Ling returned. For some reason, they were carrying animal capture poles, poles with nooses on the ends. I guess for me, if I had escaped.

"Breakfast is ready, Master, Controller," I said, careful not to show any reaction.

They stood transfixed for a moment then both begin laughing in delight.

"Potential, Minx? I think you have underestimated him and yourself."

"Why didn't you escape, M-5? You had a chance?" Minx asked.

"I didn't want to. It would have been wrong. I belong here."

"Why do you say that, M-5?"

"I want to stay with you."

She smiled. "Do you, M-5? Do you really want to stay with me?"

"Yes, Controller."

"Then, offer me your pain."

"I don't understand. I will accept the pain you give me."

"I want more from you, M-5."

Mei Ling bowed and left the room, but not without a smile at the both of us.

"Tell me. I wish to please you, Controller. How can I show you my love, my need for you?"

"Who was the woman you loved, the one you lost?" Minx asked.

I paused and took a deep breath. "She was my wife."

"What happened, Michael?"

"She died trying to have a baby. My baby. She wanted to give me a child, because she felt I was the most important person in the world. She died for me."

"And the child?" Minx asked softly.

"Died. She was five months premature. And, it was my fault."

"Why was it your fault? What did you do?"

"I didn't stop my wife from drinking. She had a problem with alcohol. She hid it from me until it was too late."

"Was she your slave? Did you own her?" Minx asked.

"No. She was free to choose. I couldn't make her stop. It would have been wrong to force her!" I protested.

"Then, it wasn't your fault. You loved her enough to let her be free to choose. You can't make a person stop drinking, or using drugs or smoking. They have to want to stop."

"I just didn't love her enough. If I had, she might have stopped!" I cried out.

"She loved you, Michael. She knew the risk; she chose the risk. She was wrong. Not you."

"I failed. She died, because I didn't stop her."

"Michael, listen to me," Minx instructed. "You are forgiven. No one is blaming you. Just yourself. You are worthy of being loved."

"Am I?" I said, crying.

"Yes, Michael, you are. And, you will be loved."

I looked up at her through the tears. She was smiling at me, love in her eyes.

"I love you."

"I know," was her sweet reply.

X

My confession of love didn't change things very much. I was still put through my exercises on the treadmill, I still slept in my little pen, and I was still hooded and collared, not allowed to roam free.

But, once a week I was led to Mei Ling's quarters and allowed to prepare dinner. I lived for those nights. I was permitted to look out the window at the sky, and after dinner Minx and sometimes Mei Ling would play with me.

She encouraged me to tell her my fantasies. She listened to my stories; she even encouraged me to sing for her. And then would come the playtime.

I learned to love being spanked by her, to take a hard whipping until my skin felt hot, to worship her feet. I wanted to do more for her. I wanted to be anything she desired me to be.

I wanted to worship her whole body. I wanted to worship her breasts, her ass, and her pussy. I wanted to suck her womanly juices from her, not just lap it from her fingers. It was becoming maddening. I couldn't think of a way to say anything like that to her. It would have been insulting at a minimum.

Then, came the night at Sin.

It was after I had served dinner to her one night. She had just requested a goblet of juice, and I had brought it to her. She ordered me to sit at her feet.

"M-5, would you like to go out with me?"

I wasn't sure I had heard her correctly.

"Go where, Controller?" I asked.

"Out. I am going to a club, and I thought you might like to come with me."

"I would be honored, Controller."

"You should be. I rarely take a pet out with me to Sin."

"Sin, Controller?"

"Yes," she smiled. "The name of the club is Sin."

It was a few nights later that I was dressed by Minx in a dark pair of pants, a white shirt, a jockstrap made of leather and a new type of collar. This one had flashing lights and small metal studs.

"Now, M-5, listen to me very carefully. If you try to escape, you will be stopped by the collar. It is designed to shock you, if you get more than thirty feet from me. Is that understood?" she explained.

"Yes, Controller."

"You will not speak to anyone or allow anyone to speak to you. You will act as if you are deaf and dumb unless I give you permission to speak."

With that she hooded me, attached a leash, and led me out.

The drive took some time, but ultimately we arrived at our destination. The hood was removed, and I found myself looking at the world again. People everywhere, noise, colors. I was actually disoriented after all the time in relative solitude.

Minx led me out of the car, and I saw that we had been in a limo. I couldn't see the driver, but I had a feeling I knew who it was.

She led me past the doorman, who bowed deeply, and into the club. We were engulfed by people and loud music. I almost panicked, but the steady pressure of the leash kept me three paces behind Minx through the main club. She led me to a door and knocked in a pattern. The door opened, and Minx led me into the room beyond.

A bondage frame was mounted on a stage at the far end of the room, and a rack of whips hung next to it.

"On stage, M-5, and remove your clothes. Keep your jockstrap on."

I did as I was told, and she secured me to the frame, face towards the back wall.

"Wait here. Do not move or speak."

She left, and a few minutes later, I could hear people entering the room. The lights dimmed, and I heard the noise die down.

Then, I heard a whip crack behind me. I jumped as well as I could, being tied. The next time, the whip cracked about my shoulder. I gasped. The strokes continued. Back, ass, legs. I could hear the people reacting to my pain. Some of them wanted me to be hit harder. But who was wielding the whip? It didn't feel like Minx's work. My tormentor stepped into my field of vision.

It was Lydia, an evil grin on her face. She stepped closer. "You should see your back, piglet. It looks like someone used a rake on it. This is the price you pay for not answering me. Remember that? You refused an order from me. You will never refuse my orders again, now will you?" she hissed in my ear.

"I obey my Controller. If she orders me to answer, I will," I murmured.

She stepped away, and I closed me eyes, waiting for the next blow to fall.

It never did. I heard Minx whispering in my ear, asking if I were all right.

"I think so, Controller, but I am really hurting."

"Do you wish to stop?"

"No, Controller. I want to make you proud of me."

"I am Michael. So very proud."

I heard her address the crowd.

"Now you have seen my slave take this whipping. He will tell you why he did it."

She turned back to me. "Tell them why you did it Michael."

"I wanted to please you."

"Louder Michael" she demanded with a stinging slap on my ass.

"I wanted to give you pleasure!" I fairly shouted.

The sound of applause built into a roar of approval.

Minx turned back to me and whispered, "You have honored me, Michael. What reward would you choose?"

"I want to lick your pussy until you cum, Controller. I want to give you physical pleasure."

"You will be granted this desire later. I promise you that. Now, I am going to untie you. You will turn, face the crowd, and bow respectfully to them. Then, you will get dressed and kneel at my feet."

"Yes, Controller." I did as I was told and looked at the crowd. Some of the people were admiring me; some seemed to pity me. I left the stage, got dressed and located Minx sitting at a table near the back of the room.

I made my way to her and knelt before her. She pulled my head into her lap and stroked it gently. I could smell her womanly juices through her dress and breathed deeply of them. I stayed there for a long time, not paying any attention to the rest of the things going on around me. They were unimportant; Minx was all important, and I wanted to bathe in her nearness. Minx was complimented many times on my performance, and she accepted the praise gracefully.

All too soon the night ended, and we made our way back to the limo. I expected to be hooded again, but was instead ordered to lie down on the floor in the back, face up.

I did and was rewarded by Minx squatting over my face.

"Now, Michael, it is time for your reward. I will give you ten minutes to make me cum. If you can not by that time, you will stop."

Without another word, she lowered her sweet wetness onto my face. My tongue darted to her clit. I nibbled it gently and sucked on it. I slid my tongue into her wet hole and lapped just under her clit, certain that would please her.

She trembled. I had found her pleasure spot. I concentrated on it. My wife had always said my oral performance was my one true talent; I hoped she was right. Minx became wetter and wetter. The cum started flowing out of her, and then I felt a sudden jerking and a moan. An orgasm. I changed my focus and slowed down for a minute, and renewed my lapping. A second orgasm, this time larger.

Then, it was over. She stopped me and ordered me to lay under her, soaking the juices into my face. I could only smell her, couldn't see her. But I thought I could hear a catlike purr from her. I hoped I was right.

XI

The ride back to, well, I guess you could call it home, seemed all too short after all of the excitement. I spent most of the ride on my back facing up. All I could see was the roof of the car and Minx sitting, enjoying the ride.

We came to a stop, and I expected to be hooded and led out of the car. Instead, Minx looked down at me, removed the collar, and ordered me to get up, get out of the car and walk forward ten paces.

I did as I was told. Above were the stars in a cold black sky and in front of me the sea of light that marked a city.

I turned and saw Minx standing by the limo, a goblet in her hand, looking at me.

"This place is special to me, M-5. I brought my first lover here and made him my slave. I have had many slaves since then, but you are the only other I have brought here."

"Why did you bring me here, Controller?"

"Because, you will be my finest creation. And, you will be my last creation."

I was flattered and startled at the same time. "Your last creation Controller?"

"Yes, M-5. You will be the last slave I train."

I knelt before her. "But, why?"

She hesitated, unsure of revealing something that perhaps I should not know. "I have other obligations I must attend to that make it impossible to continue."

She said it with a certain sadness, like a child who is told it is time to come in from playing in the warm twilight of summer.

"Minx, my Controller."

"Yes, Michael?"

"I will be your finest creation. I will show the world your skills." I indicated the goblet in her hand. "It's empty. Would you fill it for me?"

"With what, Michael?"

"I wish to drink your hot wine. Will you give me that blessing?"

Her face reflected the city neon and starlight. She removed her dress and stood clad in her garter belt, stockings, and high heels and placed the goblet on the ground below her. Facing the stars above she murmured some words I couldn't hear clearly and started pissing. Her hot liquid filled the goblet and splashed upon the ground. She stopped.

"When you drink this, you will be committed to my service in all ways. I will no longer bind you, unless it pleases me to do so. You will obey all of my commands willingly from this day forward. Do you accept this, Michael?"

I took the goblet and drank from it. It tasted bittersweet, not at all what I expected. I said nothing when I finished it, waiting for some sign from her.

She motioned me forwards and placed my face between her legs.

"Clean me, Michael."

I lapped the last traces of urine from her and withdrew.

She dressed and motioned me back into the car, saying nothing in words, but everything in her stride.

I lay down at her feet again and waited. She placed her heels upon my chest and motioned the still unseen driver to proceed with our journey. We sat in silence for the rest of the trip. I wondered whether I pleased her, worrying about things dark and unknown to me.

When we arrived, I was hooded and collared again. I was led through the night air in what seemed to be a different direction than I had traveled before. We entered a building and stopped.

The hood was removed, and I saw that I was now in a small cell with a cot. There was a basin and toilet in the cell, and a window was set into the wall.

"You will be kept here for a time, Michael. When I return, you will either be returned to your pen or you will become my body servant."

"Yes, Controller."

"And Michael," she continued. "If you become my body servant, you may call me Mistress Minx."

And she left me after locking the door of the cell.

I took advantage of the basin and washed and using the toilet was a luxury that had been denied me for some time. I stretched out on the cot to relax and fell asleep.

I was awakened by the sound of a tray sliding through the slot in the otherwise solid cell door. I ate the food and lay down again to continue my vigil. Another meal came, and then a third. Had I been waiting a full day? Under the food dish of the third meal was a note.

It is being decided.

xxx

M

Who was deciding what, though? Didn't Minx have free choice in her slaves, or was there a power over her? Perhaps, it was the same power that had said that I would be her last.

I heard a key click in the lock of the cell door. Without thinking, I ate the note. If there was a higher authority involved, I did not wish harm to come to Minx.

When the door opened, I found Lydia standing there. Her leather boots were polished and gleaming, and she wore a studded corset. In her hand was a gun. Not a normal gun, but a TASER, the kind that fires two fishhook shaped barbs into a target and sends a high voltage current into it.

"Out!" she commanded

I stepped out and knelt before her.

"You seem to be quite a troublemaker, piglet. I'm tempted to say you tried to escape, just so I can shoot you. But I won't...yet!"

She pulled a hood from her belt and tossed it at me. "Take all of your clothes off and put the hood on. Quickly!"

I obeyed her, keeping a watchful eye on her gun hand.

When hooded, she dragged me to my feet and ordered me to walk ahead of her. I was led back to the Chamber of Ay'esha, where the hood was removed, and I was pushed through the door roughly.

The room now resembled a throne room. At one end of the room was an ornately decorated chair, with lesser chairs on either side. The room was now candle lit, and music was being played softly. I could see people in the shadows watching me. I wondered who they were and what was going to happen.

"Kneel here. Do not move until ordered to," Lydia instructed. She stalked away into the shadows. I waited trying not to look around. I focused my attention on the big chair.

The music changed, became harsher. It was "Mars, God of War" from the *Planets* by Holst. As it reached the finale, a voice called out clearly for all to hear.

"The Matriarchs of Ay'esha approach! All bow and reflect on their glory!"

I averted my eyes from the dais in respect. I was going to be in the presence of the leaders of the group, the ones who even Minx obeyed.

A voice called out to me. "You are the subject known as M-5. Speak!"

"I am," I replied.

"We have been petitioned to allow your service to the woman you know as Controller Minx. Before we decide this, we will ask you to answer our questions with truth. Look upon us!"

I raised my eyes to seen Anna in the main chair, splendid in a purple robe. On her right side sat Minx and on her left, Lydia. I looked at the other women sitting on the dais. I knew some of these women from the news. There was the Wife of a President of the United States. Next to her was the Actress who became the CEO of a major studio. The Owner of a newspaper chain. There were others I did not know.

"M-5, you see before you the Matriarchs of Ay'esha. For a hundred years we have controlled the world in subtle ways. We have great power and great responsibilities. If we decide to allow your service, you will be in service to all of us. Any one of us may need to command you, and you will obey. Is that understood?"

"Yes. If I am permitted to enter into the service of Ay'esha, I will serve as needed."

"These services may not be of your liking, M-5. You may be asked to do things that are distasteful to you. You will obey even those orders?" Anna asked.

"I will obey those orders, as well."

"Even if the order is to kill someone?" Lydia demanded.

I hesitated. "No! I will not kill in cold blood."

"If they are a threat to us, you must kill them," Lydia pressed.

"You have stayed hidden from the eyes of the world for many years. Have you ever had to kill to protect your secret?" I challenged.

There was a long silence in the room. It was broken by Minx. "No. Even those who failed were not killed. They were returned to the outside world."

"And no one ever talked?" I asked.

"The world believes what it wishes to believe, M-5. Those who talked were dismissed as having perverse fantasies," Anna replied.

"Why do you wish to join in our service, M-5?" the Actress asked.

"I am in love with the Controller and wish to serve her interests."

"Love is not a reason; it is a hormonal problem," said the Owner.

"The Controller taught me to forgive myself for the death of my wife and child. She lay to rest the ghosts of my soul. I owe her my service for returning my life to me."

"It is not a debt to be repaid," said the Wife. "It is something that can not be repaid."

"And that is why I wish to enter her service. I will give everything I can as a token."

"M-5, you know that the Controller will leave someday. She has told me of your fear of being abandoned again. She will leave eventually, and this can not be changed," Anna said.

"I will be hers for the time I have with her. I learned that from my wife. We had six and a half years. I will cherish the time I have with the Controller. And perhaps when she leaves, she will give me to another who wishes a well trained pet."

There was a silence that seemed to be eternal. I waited for the next question.

"M-5, crawl to us and kneel before the Controller," Anna ordered.

I crawled across the room, head down. When I reached Minx, I placed my head at her feet.

"Controller Minx, you have heard the answers from this person. Do you wish to accept him into your service?" Anna intoned.

I felt Minx's hand on my bowed head, and then she raised my head, so I could see her face.

"I accept the service of Michael for as long as time permits. He is mine!"

"Michael, do you enter into this service of your own accord, with perfect love and perfect trust?" Anna continued.

"With perfect love, and perfect trust," I said softly.

"By the powers of Ay'esha and Astoreth, I declare this slave as bonded. So mote it be!"

XII

I was led to Minx's living quarters for the first time. Her rooms were much like Mei Ling's rooms, with the exception of the bed and a piano. The bed was a masterpiece of art. It was a wrought iron four-poster bed. At the corner posts were rings suitable for binding hands and feet in place. It was overhung by a silk canopy that seemed almost too female in comparison to the black iron of the bed. The pillows were black silk as were the sheets.

"Michael, you will sleep on the floor at the foot of the bed. You will find a pillow and quilt in the closet. You will find the kitchen is identical to the one in Mei Ling's quarters. You may use the courtyard in the morning and evening for your exercise program."

"I will prepare a copy of my schedule, and you will follow the instructions on it. When I am not here, you will stay in these rooms. You may listen to music, or if you will tell me what you like to read, I will give you one book a week."

I nodded.

"You will collect my laundry and place it in the bin in the bathroom by noon. Clean clothes and linens will be returned by six. I will give you a pair of shorts and a shirt to start with. As needed, you will be given more clothing. You will keep them in the cabinet marked for your use. Do you have any questions?"

My head was spinning from the events that had just taken place. "Yes Mistress. Should I eat with you or by myself?"

"If I am going to be out, you should eat without me. You will stay on your diet until I say otherwise. If I am here, you will serve me, and then wait for permission to eat. I will tell you if you are to eat in the kitchen or with me. I will want a shopping list from you on Sundays."

I was happy that she allowed me to dine with her.

"You will be paid for your service to me. I will keep track of the amount you have earned. Those funds may be used to purchase items for your personal pleasure."

It had not occurred to me I'd be paid.

"And, one other thing. You will not masturbate without my permission or outside of my presence. You will perform for me alone. Is that clearly understood?"

"Yes, Mistress." I had expected this.

"Good. Now go into the kitchen and fix a meal for me. I shall expect your best effort, Michael."

Her kitchen was well supplied, so fixing a good meal wasn't a problem. My problem was a good dessert. I had to do something special. I served the main portion of her meal and asked permission to return to the kitchen to fix dessert.

"What kind of dessert, Michael?"

"I don't know yet, Mistress. I need to know what you like."

"I like fruit. I like chocolate. I like most sweet things."

"Thank you, Mistress. I have an idea now. May I proceed?"

"Yes. Amaze me."

Sweet, chocolate, fruit. What did I have to work with? I found cocoa powder and sugar. Then, I spotted a basket of strawberries in the refrigerator.

A few minutes later, I presented Minx with chocolate dipped strawberries.

She got up from her chair and moved to lie on the divan. "Feed me your gift, Michael."

I sat next to the divan and held a strawberry over her mouth, so she could nibble at it. She nibbled it up to the stem and sucked the chocolate from my fingers.

"Another."

She nibbled the fruit away again, sucking on my fingers. Each time, I felt myself become more aroused by the sucking. I became more and more erect. She paid no attention to my growing erection and demanded another berry. I fed it to her. By the time the six berries were consumed, I was in painful arousal.

She glanced down at my hard prick and casually mentioned that it was somewhat impressive. "Perhaps I should tie it so that it stays that way."

"Please," I begged.

"Please what, Michael?"

"Please let me cum, Mistress," I stammered.

"No, I don't think so. Not yet. I have something special in mind for you tonight." She got up from the divan and stood over me. "You know tonight is our wedding night in a way. I think we need to make it something to remember. Go into the kitchen and wait until I call you. If you have not eaten yet, please do so."

I followed her orders and ate my dinner. I had just finished cleaning up when she called for me.

I entered the room to find it lit by candle light. A Mozart concerto was playing softly. I could see a shape in the shadows near the bathroom door.

She stepped into the light, and I saw her clearly.

She was dressed in a white satin corset, a white garter belt and stockings, and white high heels. Her hair flowed over her shoulders, and her lips were painted bright red.

And, hanging between her legs was a dildo.

"I'm going to take your ass cherry tonight, Michael. Will you give it to me?" Her voice hardened, "Or, must I take it from you?"

I was apprehensive. I feared I could not take that size dildo in me. I didn't wish to disappoint her. I swore my obedience, and I keep my word.

"It is yours to take Mistress," I said.

"On the bed, Michael, and lay on your back. I want you to see my cock slide into you."

I did as ordered and lay back waiting for her. She stepped towards the bed and placed cushions under my ass to raise it. She straddled my chest and placed her cock in my face.

"Kiss it, Michael. Tell me how much you want to be fucked by me. Beg for it, my slave."

I ran my tongue over the head of the cock that would soon be entering me. I took it into my mouth for a moment. "I want your cock, Mistress. I want you to use me for your pleasure." "Do you want me to fuck you? Tell me. Say the words."

"Fuck me, Mistress. Please take my virgin ass for your pleasure. Make me your slut!"

"Why would I want to fuck a slut like you? Tell me that," she demanded.

"Because, I can please you, Mistress. I'll be a good fuck toy for you."

"Suck my cock, slut!"

She shoved it deeper in my mouth. It tasted like her juices. I sucked on it and took it deeply into my throat.

"Oh, yes, throat my dick, bitch boy!" she moaned.

After a few more minutes she pulled it out of my mouth and to the foot of the bed. She lubricated the dildo and mounted me.

"Now my pussy boy, you will please your Mistress."

She slid the dildo into my ass. I felt her slide it in all the way up to the base. It didn't hurt like the dog tail had. She humped up against me, and I felt the base of my cock get wet from her juices. My cock became hard again. The pain faded as she pumped up against me. I became more aroused than I had been earlier. I could see the pleasure grow in her. We became one mass of pleasure. She came, shuddering against me and collapsed on my chest, gasping in relief. After a moment, she withdrew her cock from my steaming ass and unstrapped it. She dropped it on the floor and mounted me again, rubbing her wet pussy against my hard cock.

My cock sent its contents spewing up her belly and onto my chest.

She looked down at the cum on her belly and pointed at it. "Lick it off me slave."

She moved to straddle my chest. I licked the sticky mass off her belly and lapped gently at her navel.

"That's enough. Now, roll over on your side and put your hands over your head."

She got off me as I rolled over, and with a silken cord, bound my hands and attached them to a bed ring.

"Good night, Michael."

"Good night, Mistress." I had served her well.

XIII

I awoke near sunrise, with Minx still curled up against my back. It was a feeling I had not experienced in years. When you have lived alone for many years without the comfort of a partner, even being touched has a special meaning.

She stirred slightly and snuggled in closer to me. I closed my eyes and returned to sleep, thinking of the luck that had brought her to me.

When I awoke the next time, she was no longer in bed with me, and my hands had been untied. I quickly got up and went into the kitchen to make her breakfast.

I found a note taped to the stove.

Slave,

I will be out today and will return this evening. You will prepare a meal for me to be served at half past seven. You will be checked at noon by one of the other Mistresses. Be prepared to serve her as she desires.

M

I looked at the clock. It was almost noon. I hurried through my chores and made the bed with fresh sheets. I had just finished putting the clothes in the laundry basket when the door was unlocked and opened.

A short black woman entered the room. She was dressed in leather pants and a white silk top. Her boots clicked on the hardwood of the floor as she walked towards me holding a short crop.

I dropped to my knees and lowered my head in respect.

"Well," she said in a musical voice. "At least you know how to show respect for your betters. I was sent to check on you by Mistress Minx. I am Master Melody, and you will serve me today. Do you understand?"

Keeping my head down, I answered, "Yes Mistress."

She swung the crop across my back, leaving a searing pain. "You will address me as Master, slave."

"Yes, Master."

Another swing of the crop, but this time the other way.

"Master Melody, sir!" she barked.

"Yes, Master Melody, sir!" I repeated.

She walked away a few paces and turned back to me. "Well, boy, keep up with me. Heel!"

I scrambled to her side on all fours and followed, being careful to match her pace. She led me around the room a few times and indicated I should follow her out the door into the passage way.

The passageway floor was a mosaic of stone that made it difficult to stay in step without cutting my hands and knees. She led me to another door and through it.

The room was well decorated with African paintings and carvings. There was a low bed in one corner with ornate wood carvings decorating the frame. Next to it was short table and a stool.

"Get on the bed, boy!"

I lay down on the bed as directed and waited.

She sat down on the stool and open a drawer inset into the table. From it she took a cock ring, a package of cigarettes and a cigarette holder.

"Play with yourself boy, and when you're hard, put the cock ring on."

I did as I was told, although getting an erection under her steady gaze was difficult at best.

When I was aroused enough to suit her, I put the cock ring on and waited.

"Put your arms over your head and keep them there. If you move them I'll have to punish you. And I'd enjoy that, but you wouldn't," she directed.

I raised my arms exposing my armpits and chest for her.

"Hmmm, not much hair on that chest, but more than enough for my purposes elsewhere," she commented.

She placed a cigarette in the holder and lit it. Taking a puff, she removed the holder from her mouth and moved the glowing tip of the cigarette towards me. I held as still as I could. She moved it closer to my chest, and then placing the hot tip on my few chest hairs, she burned them off.

The hair sizzled from the heat. I held my breath trying to avoid the same sort of sizzle from my bare flesh.

She withdrew the holder and took another puff of smoke, heating it up again. Slowly, she moved it towards my armpits. I could see the hot ash moving towards me. It moved out of my sight, and I felt the heat as more hair was singed from my body. I started quivering from the fear.

"Making you nervous, boy? I'm very good at this. In fact, I do all of the brandings here. Perhaps I should suggest to your Mistress that you be branded," she teased.

Another puff, and the process was repeated on the other side.

Then, she moved towards my cock and balls. My erection tried to collapse, but the ring held it firm.

"Don't move, boy, or I might do some damage that would annoy your Mistress. And you can be sure that I'd blame you for it!" She moved the point of flame towards my balls. I could feel the heat radiating from it. I could see the intent look on her face as she moved it closer to my cock. I felt a slight stinging as she singed the new growth of hair around the base of it.

"Tell me what you'd do to keep me from putting it on your cock? I'd love to touch it to the tip of your dick. Convince me not to," she suggested.

"Please," I begged. "I'd do anything you wanted. I'd lick your boots, kiss your feet. Worship your ass."

"But for now, I think I'd like you to suck my hard black dick."

She ordered me to kneel in front of the stool. Removing a black dildo from the drawer, she placed it between her legs. Lighting another cigarette, she forced my mouth over the hard rubber.

"Suck my dick!"

I sucked on it and licked it as she smoked. I took it down my throat as I had the night before. I tried to be a slut for Master Melody. She just watched my pathetic efforts to behave as a whore and smoked silently.

When she finished, she pulled my head away from the dildo.

"You are useless as a cocksucker. You'd better improve before we turn you out. The first client you give that bad a blow job to will kick your ass. Then, your Mistress will kick it again when you come back without any money. You are going to be a whore for us, boy. Remember that."

She slapped my still erect cock with her hand.

"You keep that cock ring on until your Mistress removes it. Now follow me!"

The return trip was worse with my aching erection slapping on the rock of the floor every two or three feet. Master Melody led me back to Minx's room, ordered me inside and locked the door behind me.

I was left with an aching cock, scraped knees, and a sense of foreboding for my next encounter with Master Melody.

XIV

It seemed a longer day than it was by the time Mistress Minx returned to our rooms.

I had prepared eggplant parmigiana for her dinner and served it to her with some pasta. She picked at her food, and she seemed distracted.

I finally summoned up the courage to ask her if I could be of any assistance.

"No, Michael. It is nothing that your abilities can resolve." She got up from the table and ordered me to clear the dishes away.

When I returned to the room, she was sitting at her desk writing. I knelt near the kitchen door and waited so as not to distract her from her task.

She turned and saw me waiting and ordered me to kneel next to her. I moved to her side and knelt again.

Time passed and I had almost nodded off in my kneeling position when she spoke to me.

"Michael, perhaps you can be of assistance to me in this matter. Are you willing to try?"

"Yes, Mistress. Whatever I can do to help."

She frowned and warned me that her request might prove somewhat dangerous to me.

"I will not order you to do me this service, but if you are willing to help, despite some risk to yourself, I would be pleased."

"Mistress, I want to make you happy. What must I do to help?"

She stood and started pacing the room. "There are many aspects of Ay'esha that you know little about. There are forces internal to us that disagree with the methods of the Matriarchs. There are forces that believe that men should be eliminated, rather than trained to do our bidding."

"Mistress Lydia has given me that impression, Mistress," I said quietly.

She turned to face me and stopped. "You are not in any position to venture an opinion, M-5. Remember that! Nevertheless, you are correct. She does represent a faction that has very little use for men other than breeding stock."

"What can I do to help, Controller?"

She waited for a moment and told me what she desired. "I would like you to serve Lydia tonight, Michael. In any way she might wish you to serve."

I was taken aback. Serve Lydia? Lydia had made it clear that I was on her shit list, possibly even literally.

"If you please, Controller, might I ask why?"

"Without going into detail, she has suffered a personal loss. As you have also suffered the loss of a loved one, you may be able to help her at this time."

I weighed the pros and cons in my mind. If I could make Lydia a friend, it would be to my good, and apparently the good of the whole. The other side of course was the possibility of permanent physical damage. I was still aching from Master Melody's treatment. Well, I've never been known for being sensible about things like this anyway.

"Mistress, the needs of the many out weigh the needs of the few or the one. 'Tis a far, far better thing I do, than I have even done before.'"

"The Dickens quote is unnecessary, although I am pleased to find you literate. Just remember the last part of the line please."

I searched my memory. "'Tis a far better resting place than I have ever known before…"

I was led hooded and tied to Lydia's quarters. The cock ring was still in place from earlier, so I was displayed somewhat more than usual.

I could hear my Mistress speaking to Lydia in quiet tones before

Lydia spoke to me.

"You wish to serve me piglet?" she demanded.

"Yes, Mistress, I do. I wish to give you pleasure," I assured her.

"I am in a very bad mood, piglet. You know how much I want to hurt you. Do you still want to serve me?"

"Yes, Mistress."

"Were you ordered to serve me, piglet?"

"No, Mistress. I am doing this willingly," I answered.

She spoke to Minx quietly, and then Minx spoke to me. "Michael, you will obey Lydia as you obey me, and you will keep our discussion of Dickens in your mind. Lydia will return you when she is through with you."

I heard Minx walk away, leaving me to my fate. I could hear nothing from Lydia.

I stood, cloaked in darkness, the apprehension growing every second that passed.

Then, the slash of a whip down my spine. I felt the warm trickle of blood running down my back. Another lash across the shoulders, driving me to my knees. I could her Lydia breathing. I could feel her anger and hate radiating like a furnace scorching me. Another blow across my exposed ass. I felt another trickle of blood on me. Or, was it blood? Another blow and yet another. The pain was becoming extreme. My fear grew into full bloom. I rolled on the floor trying to escape her fury. She was a raging inferno. Then, the blows seemed to reduce in force, as they dropped off. I could feel the wetness on my skin again.

The sound of her breathing became more labored until I knew what caused it. The wetness was her tears as she cried in anger. But not with anger at me, but the universe that had hurt her.

I fought back my pain. She was hurting far worse than I was. I knew her pain, the pain of grievous loss.

"Mistress Lydia, please let me help you," I said through shaking lips.

"Help me?" she screamed. "What presumption! I don't need your help! I don't need anything from you other than your blood!"

"Here, take it," I offered. "I am here to please you."

I rolled onto my hands and knees with my ass up and waited for the next blows. I knew I couldn't take much more, I could only hope that I would pass out.

The next blow never came.

For the first time when she spoke to me, the hatred was gone from her voice, leaving only the anger. "You are willing to let me beat you bloody?"

"I am not willing, but I will do it to please you," I said respectfully.

"Why? You are a fool, if you do that."

"I was asked by my Mistress, if I was willing to serve you, and I agreed. She said I might be hurt, and I agreed."

"Why would you do that?" she demanded.

"Because, you needed someone."

"What do you know of need?" she demanded.

"You have suffered a loss of some kind today. I wished to help."

There was a thoughtful silence

"If you know that, then you know too much."

Mistress Minx had said it might be dangerous, not lethal.

There was another silence, then the hood was removed and she looked at me with puzzlement. "You wish to help me? You know how much I hate you and your kind, and yet you want to help me. How amusing. I don't want your help or your pity. Get out of my sight before I decide to do something about your insolence. Go into the kitchen and remain there until your Mistress comes for you."

I did as I was bidden, and a short time later Minx came into the kitchen. She stopped when she saw the welts and blood on my body. For the first time, I saw hatred in her eyes.

"You permitted Lydia to do this to you, Michael?" she demanded.

"I was not given a choice, Mistress. She left me tied as you see me here."

"We will speak of this later. For now, I am taking you back to your pen. Perhaps a night in a cage again will remind you that you must not be injured, or you will be unable to serve us."

She took a hood from a pocket and placed it over my head. As she led me out, I heard her ask Lydia if I had been entertaining enough for her.

"He was insolent, so I punished him. I don't need or want his help. Or, yours. Now get out!"

Minx said nothing and led me out of the room and back to the cage I had first been confined in. I crawled into the cage and collapsed on the padding exhausted from my ordeal.

"You will spend the night here Michael. In the morning I will treat your wounds. I must see Anna right now. I will lock the door so you will not be disturbed."

She left the room after locking the cage, and I heard the door to the room lock. I was again in darkness, both physically and mentally. What had I done wrong? Why was Minx angry, and why did she need to see Anna?

Was Minx going to get rid of me? I wept in my pain and misery. I didn't want to go away. I didn't mean to disappoint her. I fell asleep with a heavy heart.

I awoke to Minx's voice.

"You see how much damage was done to him?"

"He agreed to serve Lydia. The choice was his. And if she wished to beat him, it was her choice," said Anna.

"It is not her right to damage my property to the point of being unusable. He agreed to do this for a reason beyond pleasing me."

"Oh, and what might that reason be?" Anna asked.

I stirred and turned as best as I could in my cage toward the voices.

"The needs of the many outweigh the needs of the few or the one," I murmured.

There was a startled silence.

"Repeat yourself Michael," Anna commanded.

"The needs of the many outweigh the needs of the few or the one," I repeated louder.

"So, you did this for Ay'esha, not for your Mistress?" Anna pressed.

"I serve both by serving either. I agreed to serve in order to be with Mistress Minx. I will pay the price demanded."

There was another silence.

"Take him to the examining room Minx. Have Mei Ling start the treatment for his pain. I will send Ruth to tend to his wounds. When Ruth arrives, you will join me in my chambers. I wish to discuss this matter in private."

XV

I was released from my cage and unbound. My Mistress led me back to the examining room and removed the hood. She assisted me onto the table as Mei Ling arrived with her box.

"He is to be relieved of his pain, Mei Ling. Please proceed quickly," Minx said.

"I'm a patient patient," I said.

That earned a look of dismay from the both of them.

"Please make sure that Ruth examines him for brain damage," Minx said.

Mei Ling shook her head. "If he is aware enough to make a pun than bad, then his brain is fine. His mind is another matter."

"Now, Michael, I am going to start inserting the needles. Close your eyes and breathe as I tell you," she instructed. "In deeply."

There was the sting, then the warm glow.

"Breath out all the way."

Again the sting, then the warmth.

My mind started drifting as the pain flowed away. Time slowed down. I only dimly noticed another person entering the room. It didn't seem to matter much. From a far off distance I could hear Minx and Mei Ling speaking to the newcomer. The distance became shorter as I felt the pain return in short bursts until I was back to earth.

"Michael, this is Ruth. She is a doctor and will attend to your wounds. I must go now," Minx said. She turned and left me.

I saw Ruth was an older woman. She had a twinkle in her eye as she examined me.

"Well, I see that you have been playing too rough. Moderation is the key to success, my boy. Remember that the next time," she said in a soft English accent.

"If I have a choice, Doctor, I will avoid excess," I said politely.

"You were not given a choice about this. That is not good."

"Well, I was in a way. Did you ever watch cartoons when you were young, Doctor?" I asked.

She chuckled softly. "Young man, I am an aunt. I have watched more cartoons with my nieces and nephews than you have ever seen."

"'If you're afraid you'll have to overlook it; besides you knew the job was dangerous when you took it.'"

She laughed. "You will have a large number of bruises, and you have some whip marks that I shall have to sew up. But overall, you will recover in a reasonable amount of time. I would say a week, and you will be as good as new."

"A week? I need to be able to serve my Mistress, Doctor. Is there anyway to speed up my recovery?"

"I believe you said 'I'm a patient patient' earlier. Things do heal in time. And after treatment this severe, rest is my prescription. I will also prescribe some pain medication."

"No, Doctor. I would prefer not to use them," I said firmly.

She looked at me sternly. "You are refusing my treatment? Remember what you are. Doctors orders, my boy."

Mei Ling interrupted at that point. "With all due respect, Doctor, I will treat him for pain. He is strong willed for a slave. If he feels that drugs would interfere, then he should not use them. My methods are not addictive. I have some herbals that will provide relief without interfering with his mind."

Ruth snorted. "Witch doctors, stuff and nonsense. I still don't understand why you persist in using potions like some old hag."

Mei Ling smiled. "Doctor, please remember that my ancestors were decadent while yours were still staining themselves blue."

Ruth regained her dignity and nodded curtly to me. "Roll over so that I can start on your back. Mei Ling, if you would assist me, I can finish quicker."

The doctor was fast and precise. Despite her insulted attitude, she was gentle as she could be with my wounds.

"If you will take care of yourself, you won't even be able to tell you were beaten after a month," she said as she finished.

"I shall report his condition to Anna and Minx. You will see to his care from this point on?" she said to Mei Ling.

"I shall take responsibility for him, Doctor."

"Doctor," I called. "Thank you for your help. I hope I may do you a service at some time."

She turned back and a smile crossed her face. "Grow strong and serve your Mistress. That's reward enough for me."

She departed, leaving me with Mei Ling.

"She is right you know. Pain interferes with healing. My potions will not give you the same level of relief that her medicines will," she advised.

"I would prefer to try and control the pain in other ways. I have never liked drugs."

"You fear having your mind tampered with? You have never been drunk?" she asked.

"I was medicated for a kidney stone once. I was very uncomfortable with the results."

"What medicine was used?"

"They used a form of Demerol. But they gave it to me after a dye injection to locate the stone."

"I understand. The medicine had no time to be absorbed, but traveled to your brain instantly."

"It was like being hit with an iron bar. One moment I was in moderate pain, the next, you could have shot me, and I wouldn't have cared. It scared me losing that much control. I don't drink, smoke or use drugs. It's just the way I am. My profession required clear thinking."

"What did you do before Minx brought you to us?" she asked curiously.

"I was a computer man. I programmed computers, fixed them and taught computer skills for a large company," I said. "I was just wondering if anyone has even noticed my absence."

"Perhaps, they have. Perhaps, not. Roll onto your back again. I will be back in a few minutes with some medicine for you," she said.

She left the room, and I lay there thinking about my life. Did anybody even know I was gone? It occurred to me that my house was sitting abandoned. For the first time, I started regretting my choice to stay.

Mei Ling returned with a goblet of liquid and helped me to sit up so I could drink. It was like a tea, but more bitter. She watched me as I drank it all and warned, "You will feel lightheaded at first, but the effect will soon pass."

She was right. It felt like my head was detaching, and then everything sharpened into a clear focus. Things became more colorful and the sound of her voice seemed to change. I felt very good, too good. I realized too late that there was something in the tea.

I tried to get up and found that I couldn't move. I tried to speak and found myself unable to do so.

"I have wanted to try this mixture on someone for quite a while now. I formulated it myself. It is designed to cause a temporary paralysis in the nervous system. You can still hear and see, but you can't move."

She noticed my cock ring and removed it. The area around my balls was purple from trapped blood. "If you were not in this state, you would be screaming in agony as the blood returned."

She was right. The pain was like creeping fire up my groin. I could only sit helpless as the feeling slowly burned itself out.

She watched carefully as the blood returned to my swollen groin. "We used something like this to capture you, with a compound to render you unconscious," she said. "It has proven useful on many occasions."

She sat and watched me, checking my pulse at intervals. After a time, I started feeling a tingling sensation. Slowly, I returned to normal, except the pain was absent. I felt truly normal again.

"Did your test give you pleasure, Master?" I asked as soon as my voice returned.

"Yes, it did, Michael. You are not angry about being tricked?" she asked.

"Yes, I am, but you did say you would relieve my pain. Your potion did do that as it wore off. I feel much better now."

"Very good. We will repeat this treatment as needed. For now, I will return you to your room to await your Mistress."

XVI

Mei Ling returned me to Minx's quarters and removed the hood. My ordeal must have lasted for hours, because I could see daylight through the half open kitchen door.

I asked her if I could serve her breakfast, and she assented.

I returned to the main room with the food and found that Minx had returned. There was fire in her eye and anger in her voice when she saw me.

"Kneel, now!" she demanded.

I dropped the tray with a clatter and knelt where I was. Minx walked towards me with deliberate steps, a crop in her hand. It was like being stalked by a cat, and I was for sure the mouse.

She stood over me and looked down. "You are undoubtedly the stupidest slave I have ever owned! Don't you have any instinct for self preservation at all? You might have been killed, you fool! You just wait until you heal, because after you do, I'm going to beat your sorry ass until it's bruised again!"

I listened, head down, as the storm continued to rage.

"I have devoted time and effort in you, too much to see you throw it away. Do you see yourself as that much of an object? Answer me!"

"I was just trying to follow my orders," I stammered.

"Your orders and your oath of obedience do not require that you die. When you have reached your limits, beg for mercy. Even Lydia will listen at that point, shit for brains!"

She turned to Mei Ling. "Take him into the bathroom and chain him face down in the tub. And don't be gentle about it!"

Mei Ling grabbed my arm, twisted it behind me, lifted me to my feet, and marched me into the bathroom. The bathtub was a sunken tub of black marble, twice the width of a normal tub. Inset into the corners were restraint rings. She pushed me face down into the tub and stood on my neck as she attached chains to my wrists and legs. I felt the cold marble on my body as my face was pressed into the stone.

I heard Minx's voice from above me. "Now slave, let's see if you have learned anything."

The water started flowing. It slowly crept up towards my face. I tried to raise my head to stay ahead of it, but the force of Mei Ling's foot held me down. The margin of space for air shrank slowly.

"Mistress, please." I said as the water crept up.

"Please what?" came from far above me.

"Mercy, Mistress," I begged.

"No. You have a lesson to learn first."

The water crept over my nose forcing me to breath through my mouth as well as I could.

"Mercy, Mistress," I burbled through the water.

"No."

I gasped a last lung full of air as the water covered my whole face. I held my breath as long as I could. The pressure on my neck lifted, and I raised my head enough to breathe out and suck in more air. With the pressure removed, I could breathe through my mouth, but that space was waning.

"Mercy, Mistress," I panted.

"Why?" she demanded.

"Please," I begged.

"It amuses me to see you this way. Why should I stop? It might please me to drown you," she asked.

I was submerged again, before I could answer her.

A strong hand pulled my head up by the hair. "Tell me why I should stop." "Because, you may want to use me again. Please, Mistress."

The water stopped, and then started draining away.

"Good boy, but I want you to answer one question for me. Tell me the truth. Why didn't you beg for mercy from Lydia?" she asked quietly.

"Because, I wanted you to be proud of me. I wanted to take it to please you. I should be able to take what is done to me. I didn't want to fail you. I'm sorry I did."

"You didn't fail me. You failed only yourself, Michael. You will see many slaves do things that you physically or mentally can't do. I only ask that you try. Do not be ashamed of failure or feel badly that you can't do something another can. Take pride in what you can do to serve me. Remember that I love you. As your wife loved you and accepted you, so do I. You must learn to trust again."

She released my head and walked away leaving me to think on the cold wet marble, the last of the water gurgling down the drain under me. She was right, of course. It would be arrogance to assume I could do everything. There was a quote that sort of summed it up. "Some people God gave big brains, others he gave big muscles. Don't ask me to move furniture." I did want her to be proud of me, but I guess I was trying too hard. I was acting half my age, trying to impress a woman. I felt myself blush. I should know better than that. What was it the doctor had said? Moderation is the key to success.

"Why are you blushing, Michael?" Mei Ling asked, startling me. I had assumed she left with Minx.

"Because I just realized I am a fool, Master," I answered.

"You are achieving wisdom, Michael. You have realized that you are a fool. Now what do you propose to do about it?" she asked.

"I will try not to be foolish about things I have no control over, Master."

"Such as?"

"I will not try to be everything for my Mistress. I will just be what I can be for her, Master."

"The light dawns. She demands much, but accepts what is offered if it comes from the heart and spirit. Please to remember that in the future, Michael. Be worthy of her."

She patted me on the head, and I heard her leave, closing the door behind her.

XVII

It was some time before my Mistress returned and released the chains that bound me to the tub. She said nothing as she led me back into the main room. She pointed at the tray I had dropped. I quickly picked up the scattered debris and removed it to the kitchen. I returned with cleaning solution and a towel and cleaned up the grease and syrup stains from the rug.

The silence continued all of that evening until it was time for bed. It was broken only by her direction to lie down on the floor, so that she could shackle me to the foot of the bed. After chaining me and covering me, she lit a tall candle and turned out the lights.

The room was lit by the glow of the single candle. I could see her laying in bed, her black silk gown glittering in the candlelight and reflecting on her open eyes as she looked at the canopy overhead.

I watched as the candle burned down, but her eyes never closed for more than a moment. It was as if she were watching something far away, something only she could see. I wished I could touch her to see if there was anything I could do to help her. I could feel distress from her, not anger, but distress. Had I created a problem for her? No, I had created a problem for myself, but not for her.

"Mistress," I whispered.

"Yes, Michael," she replied not looking at me.

"May I be of help to you?" I asked.

"No, Michael, you have been enough help for now."

"Yes, Mistress. Good night." It was all I could say.

When the candle had burned almost to extinction, she was still awake, as was I. The pain was returning, and it was making me restless. I rolled over and moaned softly. Almost before the sound had died away, she was at my side. She took my head into her lap and stroked my hair.

"I never intended for you to suffer pain like this. I should not have asked you to try to help Lydia." She sighed.

"I wanted to help. And, I tried to do too much. I wanted to show her that a man could be something to be trusted, not hated. And, I was wrong. And, I'm paying for it," I said softly.

"As am I, Michael. I use pain to condition, not torture. I enjoy watching a slave being pushed to his limits, but not over them."

"I understand. May I ask what Anna had to say, Mistress?"

Minx looked away from me. "Anna feels that you should be sent away. She was not happy with you or me or Lydia. Lydia has been ordered to repay me for your loss of service to me while you heal. I have been ordered to punish you for your error. And I will be punished by Anna for trying to interfere."

"How will you be punished, Mistress?" I asked in dismay.

"I am to be whipped by Anna in front of the group," she said in a resigned voice. She hesitated before continuing. "And your punishment will be to have to watch."

"When?" I whispered in horror.

"At dawn, in the courtyard. Anna will come for us at that time."

I lay, head in her lap, wishing for the darkness to be eternal, never to see daylight again rather than to see her treated like a slave.

And that is how we spent the night, what might be our last night together.

Dawn crept into the room from the kitchen, its fingers reaching out to touch us with soft light.

There was a knock on the door and Anna entered, whip coiled at her belt.

"It is time, Minkin. Are you prepared for punishment?" she asked, as if by ritual.

Minx stood and removed her robe. Her proud body stood unmarked in the light, as she spoke.

"I am prepared for the punishment ordained by my sisters," she said, the courage of a lioness in her voice.

"And you, slave. Are you also prepared for this?" Anna asked me.

I started to reply, and then looked at Minx. She smiled at me, and I took courage from it.

"Yes. I am prepared to face the punishment you have ordained," I said, not taking my eyes from Minx's.

Anna unlocked the shackles from the bed and relocked them around my ankles.

"Go," she directed.

We went through the kitchen and into the courtyard beyond. A whipping post had been erected near the fountain. Anna secured Minx to the post and locked my shackles to one of the benches.

We were joined one at a time by hooded figures until there were twenty people forming a square around the post.

"Hear me, my sisters," Anna called out. "Witness the punishment meted out to our sister. Learn from her error."

Anna stepped back and uncoiled the single tail whip.

"The punishment shall be ten lashes for her misjudgment."

The first crack of the whip caused my blood to burn. Across Minx's perfect skin was a thin line of blood. The second and third lashes came. The fourth and fifth. Minx struggled to stay mute, as did I.

I wanted to scream my anger and defiance at Anna, at the group. It was my fault. Mine!
I turned away and heard the crack of the whip next to my head.

"You were ordered to watch her punishment. You defy the order?" Anna asked loudly.

I looked back at the scene. Minx, my love, my Mistress, was in pain, and I was the cause.

"No. I question its fairness. I was responsible for the problem. I should be up there, not her," I protested.

"She is responsible for you, your actions, and your mistakes. You are a dumb animal," she reminded me.

"And, you know why I did what I did. Do the rest know why I did it?" I asked.

"Your reasons are not important." She turned away and coiled the whip to strike again.

"The needs of the many," I called to the hooded figures.

One of the figures stepped forward. "Outweigh the needs."

A second figure stepped out. "Of the few."

And yet a third figure who removed her hood and looked at me. Lydia. "Or, the one."   "I did what I did to try to repay Ay'esha for permitting me to serve Mistress Minx. She returned my life to me. She felt Lydia's pain at her loss. I, too, have suffered such a loss, and she thought I might be able to help. I tried and failed. If trying to help someone in pain is to be punished, then I should be punished as well."

Lydia stared at me for a long time. "You are a fool. It is your false sense of duty that will be your destruction."

She turned to the group. "This is why we must control the males or destroy them. We do not need their help. We already have control of much of the world through our puppets. We should strike now."

Anna turned to her. "You have made your opinion quite clear in the Circle. But, I am the Mother of Many. Your methods are as crude as those of the average male, Lydia. That is why we follow the plan of the First Mother of Many."

"You have your plan, and I have mine. There are others who agree with me. Time will judge which of them is right. I shall leave Ay'esha," Lydia swore. "And you, slave. There will come a time when you will regret this meeting. I shall not kill or harm a sister, but you will pay for your foolish ways."

With a final defiant toss of her head, Lydia marched off, followed by three of the hooded figures.

Anna turned back to me with a look of sorrow on her face. It was the look of a mother sending her only child off to war. For an instant, I saw tears forming in her eyes, but then the look was replaced by one of determination. "Slave, you have caused a great disruption today. And we shall all pay the price of your folly. But what is done is done."

Anna walked towards me with her whip.

I knelt before her and waited for the lash to fall. I deserved it, and I knew it. I closed my eyes.

"I now understand why Minx loves you. You are indeed a good and rare man."

I opened my eyes to see Anna smiling gently down at me. The smile passed as she turned back to the group.

"Shall I continue to punish our sister, or will you accept the blood of her slave?" she called out.

"Blood!" replied the cloaked figures.

"You will have it. The slave will take the remainder of our sister's punishment," Anna replied.

Minx was released from the whipping post, and I was secured there instead. She looked at me as Anna lashed me to the post. "He is my slave, Anna. I shall administer his punishment." Anna looked at us and handed Minx the whip. They walked out of my vision.

"Prepare yourself, slave," my Mistress called.

I braced for the impact on my tattered back.

CRACK!

"One!" she called out.

CRACK!

"Two!"

CRACK!

"Three!"

CRACK!

I screamed as the fourth one cut across the welts of the previous night. Only one more left.

"Four!"

CRACK!

I slumped against the post sobbing. The fire of pain burned through me leaving the gray ash of numbness.

"Five!"

I waited for more. Surely I would now be punished for my errors.

"And what punishment shall we mete out to the slave for the trouble he has caused, my sisters?" Anna asked, "Is there one who will speak for him before I determine his punishment?"

"I shall," I heard Mei Ling say.

"And I," called Ruth.

"I speak for him," said Master Melody.

Other voices new to me spoke as well.

"It seems that you have won some converts, slave," Anna said as she walked toward me.

"His punishment shall be the withholding of pain medication for his wounds. Pain makes man think, thinking makes man wise, and wisdom makes life endurable!"

XVIII

As soon as the ropes were released, I slumped towards the ground, only to be caught by Ruth. She helped me into Minx's quarters and lay me down on the divan.

"If you don't wish your wounds to heal, you can always roll in broken glass," she said in an aggravated tone.

"You mean this isn't covered by insurance?" I replied weakly.

She snorted. "Lloyds of London wouldn't cover you with the foolish things you do."

Minx entered at that point and Ruth turned to her.

"He will be just fine. Except of course he's still a fool. He might live longer if you put a muzzle on him."

"Thank you, Ruth. I shall take it under consideration. As to you, Michael, I am quite able to take my own punishment, thank you," Minx replied.

Ruth bowed and left.

I looked down at the floor at that point.

"However," she continued. "I understand why you did it."

"I'm sorry, Mistress. But I didn't wish to see you punished for something I did wrong."

"Michael, when it comes to things like that, you are a dumb animal. You have no rights or responsibilities for anything. As your owner, I am totally in charge. I think that Anna may be right about you leaving, at least for a short while. Ay'esha owns a women's health spa on the coast, and I think it would be good for you to go there. You will learn how to perform massage, manicure, pedicure, and other talents suited to a body servant. And, you will learn to be discreet, because there will be women there who don't know of Ay'esha."

"Mistress, please," I begged. "Don't send me away. I love you."

"I know. And you are sworn to obey me. You will go and you will return to me. Lydia leaving will make me too busy to pay attention to you as much as I should for at least two weeks. You will leave next week after the doctor says you can travel."

"But who will take care of you while I'm gone?" I asked.

"Michael, I desire your service. I do not need it. I am quite able to take care of myself while you're gone. And when you return, you will be even better suited to serve me. And, I know you wish to do your best.

"Now," she said changing the subject, "I'm going to fix breakfast for both of us. I would like you to prove to you that I can take care of myself."

She winked at me and grabbed my apron from its hook on the door.

The rest of the week went as the weeks before had gone. I cooked and cleaned. Minx came and went as was her way, and I continued to sleep at her feet on the floor.

The day before I was to leave, I was instructed to prepare dinner for four to be served at eight o'clock sharp. I did as instructed and at exactly eight, the door opened and Minx entered followed by Mei Ling, Ruth and Anna in their most elegant gowns. Each one carried a short riding crop.

I knelt as they entered, with head bowed and waited for Minx to address me.

"Michael you may serve now."

I served the meal and knelt next to her as she indicated. There was very little conversation over dinner, and I was concerned that there was a problem with the meal. After a time, I was directed to clear the table and retire to the kitchen until called for. I took the time to clean up the kitchen and make up a shopping list of basics to restock. I knew that Minx could take care of herself, but I didn't want to leave things in a mess.

"Michael, please come in here," Minx's voice called.

I returned to the room to find the four women standing waiting for me.

"Kneel in front of me, Michael," she commanded.

I knelt and waited. The women closed in around me and stood looking down. "Look at me!"

I looked into her smiling face.

"You are about to be released into the outside world again. You must remember that if you wish to return to me, the world must remain ignorant of us," Minx reminded me.

"I promise that I will tell no one. I wish to return to you, Mistress," I affirmed.

"The temptations of the world are strong, Michael, and many women will find you desirable as you are trained now," Mei Ling spoke. "You must resist them to achieve your true desire."

"I understand, Master. But, I know who I wish to serve for the rest of my life."

She smiled down at me. "You are truly deserving of our attentions, Michael. You will find a gift in your bag from me. Use it wisely."

"Michael, you are in good health. Your time at the Spa will improve it more. Take the training that is offered and work hard. Return to us in peak condition. We have use for you," advised Ruth.

Anna took her turn. "Michael, face me."

I turned towards her and waited. From a box on the table, she removed a small golden medallion and placed it around my neck. On it was pictured a profile of a very handsome man.

"To those who know, this medallion indicates you are owned and part of Ay'esha. Until now, no member would harm you while you wore this. With Lydia's departure from our ranks, I would caution you to be wary of those you do not know be they male or female.

"You will be driven to your new location in the morning, and when it is time to return, you will be delivered to us again."

"Thank you Mother of Many for your gift and the gift of trust you have given me, as well," I said quietly.

"It is a trust you have earned by your words and actions, Michael. Ruth is correct. We have use for your abilities."

"Michael, put your head down and raise your ass," Minx ordered.

I assumed the position as instructed and waited.

Each woman in order swung their crops at my bare ass causing it to redden with each blow. After each one had delivered five swats, I was ordered to kiss the feet of each one of Minx's guests in homage to them.

I willingly kissed the feet of these women who loved me enough to help me become better.

They departed after kissing Minx goodnight.

"Now Michael," she said turning her attention to me. "We have a little time together. What would you like to do tonight?"

"I would like to make love to you tonight, Mistress. Please?" I asked shyly.

She laughed softly at the request. "Don't you think that's being a little self centered, looking for your pleasure instead of mine?"

I bowed my head in embarrassment. "Yes Mistress. I apologize."

"Michael, look at me."

I looked up to see her smiling.

"There is nothing wrong in being self centered. Being selfish is wrong. Do you wish to give me pleasure or only yourself?"

"I wanted to give you pleasure," I said.

"And you would feel no pleasure yourself?" she asked.

"I would enjoy it, yes. I like giving you pleasure."

"And you think you can give me pleasure?" she asked with the smile turning sly.

Did I? Was I actually good enough to give her the pleasure she deserved and was her right? "Yes, Mistress I do."

Her reaction surprised me, for instead of the slap I expected for my insolence, she knelt and kissed me.

Now I was really confused. She could see my confusion and took me by the hand.

"Michael, you have given me pleasure. You have served me well and protected me. I took you by force from the world and reduced you to an animal. You had lost faith in your ability to love anyone. You didn't believe you could give pleasure. And now you believe in yourself again."

She was right. For the first time since the death of my wife, I wasn't filled with doubts or worries. I wasn't such a bad guy after all. If someone like Minx, who could have any man she wanted, loved me, I must be special.

Minx saw the change as I realized what she had been trying to teach me. "Yes Michael, you are special. You are my slave. Mine and no one else's. I own you totally, and that is what you desire. To be owned by me."

She took the crop from the table and toyed with it, watching my reaction.

"I will take pleasure from you tonight, slave. Pleasure in your submission to my will and desires. Lie down on the floor on your back and close your eyes. Arms at your sides!"

I obeyed my Mistress and Owner, the one who loved me. She Who Must be Obeyed.

There was a momentary pause, I heard her walk away from me. My mind wandered as I waited. What new pleasure would she take from my submission? I felt a weight on my chest followed by something hot dripping on me. It burned.

"Do not move, slave. No matter what, do not move."

I lay as still as possible. There was a feather light touch on my ribs that made me flinch. The burning sensation returned, only this time in multiple locations. I held back a moan. The touch continued almost maddeningly. I wanted to cry out. She knew what pain tickling caused me. I tried to ignore it. I forced myself to think of other things, to deaden myself against the assault on my senses. The touching continues and with it the spasms that caused the burning sensation. I could smell now what caused it. The candelabra from the table rested on my chest, with its candles burning low.

The touching moved to my feet with no effect. Since breaking a leg, a light touch on my feet could not be felt at all. The sensation increased in pressure, with no change in my reaction. I was dead from the feet up. Then, there was a solid slap across my feet with the crop that sent the wax spattering even though I held as still as possible. I did moan at that point from the wax and the sting of the crop.

The weight of the candelabra was removed from my chest, and I took in a deep breath.

"Open your eyes, slave," Minx commanded.

I did, and from my limited viewpoint, I could see wax all over my chest and belly, matting the newly grown hair.

"Now I can remove that hair from you. I prefer you hairless," she said taking a grip on a patch of the wax. She yanked sharply, and I gasped. Another patch, another yank. The pain swelling, and silently retreating. She took her time and pleasure in the task of denuding my chest. When she was done, she ordered me onto the bed, where she restrained my hands and feet to the metal rings.

She removed her evening gown and threw it onto the divan. She stood dressed much as I had first seen her on that first night, so long ago it seemed. The black corset shimmered in the candlelight, and the boots shone in the glow.

The crop in her hand seemed less an item of torture and more a badge of honor now. I had won the battle with myself. I loved Mistress Minx.

XIX

I was being delivered to the Spa by an unmarked van, blindfolded, with only my clothes, a travel bag, and a gold medallion that I toyed with nervously.

It would be my first real taste of freedom since that night when I had become the captive of an organization led by women. I had been broken in spirit by the death of my wife many years before and was restored by the efforts of a woman I knew only as Mistress Minx. I was to be trained to serve others now, but my real love remained with her. I hoped that I would be able to return soon to her side.

It was her decree that I should become better trained in body service and the Spa, owned by the organization I knew as Ay'esha, was the best place.

My thoughts were interrupted by the van slowing down and making a sharp turn. We proceeded down an incline, and I could smell salt air and hear the ocean surf. We braked to a halt and the engine was turned off. The voice of a woman I did not know instructed me to remain seated until someone came for me. The driver's door opened and closed. There was a short delay and the side door of the van was opened and the blindfold was removed.

I found myself looking at a giantess of a woman, over six feet tall and powerfully built.

"You are the new trainee?" she asked, looking me over carefully.

I nodded, being unsure as to permission to speak.

"Speak up! You were sent here for training?" she repeated.

"Yes, Ma'am. My name is --" I started to say.

"Your name is of no concern here. A name will be assigned to you for the duration of your stay, and you will respond to it only. Is that understood clearly?" she barked.

"Yes, Ma'am," I replied quickly.

"Very well. Bring your things and follow me. I want to examine you before I assign you to a duty post."

I looked around before following her and could see that the building was almost a Spanish or Italian fortress by way of design. Looking behind me, I could see a fence and a guard post at the top of the bluffs near the road that I had come down in the van.

I followed her across the driveway and down a flight of stairs into the lower floor of the building. She led me down the hallway and into a medical examining room at the end of the hall.

"Put your things down and strip. I want to take some measurements," she ordered.

I did as told and stood while she used a tape measure to check my pant and shirt sizes.

"On the scale."

I was actually grateful for the diet that my Mistress had placed me on as the Giantess examined me intently.

"Normal. The scars on your back are healed and the medical report that was sent to me before you arrived indicates you are in acceptable shape."

"Thank you, Ma'am"

She slammed her fist down on the examining table. "Acceptable is not good enough! When you leave here, you will be in exceptional shape. You will lift weights, you will run, and you will take part in our self defense classes. I intend to run your ass off, slave. Is that a problem for you?"

"Ma'am, no, ma'am!" I replied loudly. I knew my place, and it wasn't very high around here.

She blinked at my response. "Very well, slave. You are aware that not all of the guests here are members of Ay'esha. You will therefore speak to no one without permission from me, or someone I personally designate. And I mean nobody! Clear?"

"Ma'am, no, ma'am!"

Her tone softened a bit. "I will have someone escort you to your quarters. When not in training or on duty, you will stay there until I say otherwise. Questions?"

"No, ma'am."

She left the room, and I sat down on the examining table to wait for my escort to arrive.

It gave me time to reflect on my situation. The tune that kept running through my head was "You're in the Army Now." Sigh!

My musical musings were interrupted by the arrival of a well-tanned young woman in shorts and T-shirt.

"Hi. You must be Charles. I'm Katy. The Queen sent me to escort you to your room," she said, holding out her hand.

I shook her hand and nodded in answer to her question.

"Grab your stuff and c'mon. It's just upstairs from here."

I picked up my bag and started to follow her, but was stopped by her giggle.

"Maybe you should get dressed first," she suggested.

I would have been embarrassed, but after the time spent in Mistress Minx's service, I had become accustomed to being nude. The Mistress was right in sending me here. I needed to relearn the conventions of society.

I dressed quickly, not sparing Katy more than a cursory glance, and followed her down the hall and up the stairs.

My room was actually quite nice, with a window, a real bed, and even a small bathroom. A major change was the presence of a telephone sitting on a small desk.

"You'll find your schedule on the desk. I'll come back at six to escort you to dinner," Katy advised.

I bowed towards her, and she smiled.

"You don't talk much do you?' she asked.

I pointed to my mouth and motioned as if pulling a zipper.

"Ah, one of those people," she said in sudden understanding. "Don't worry I won't tell anybody."

With that, she left the room, and I heard the lock click behind her. I thought about what she had said. *One of those people.* I knew I wasn't the first to be sent here, but were there others here now?

I had about an hour according to the clock on the wall, before she returned. I used the time to clean up and change into fresh clothes. An examination of the schedule called for my day to begin at six in the morning and last until six at night.

At exactly six, Katy unlocked the door and invited me out. I stepped into the hall, and she took my arm and led me to the far end of the hall and through a door.

The dining area reminded me of a school cafeteria in design, right down to the steam table at the end of the room. Katy escorted me to the serving line and placed items on my tray as I indicated them by pointing.

When I was finished, she led me to a table already occupied by about half a dozen other people.

"Everybody, this is Charles. He's taken a vow of silence, so he can't answer questions," Katy explained.

Well, that made as much sense as the truth anyway.

"I'm Neils Pederson. I'm in charge of water safety," he said with a slight Danish accent and holding out his hand.

I shook it and was glad to still find all of my fingers afterwards.

A slim older woman with reddish hair was next to offer me a hand in greeting. "I'm Emma. I'm the self defense instructor here," she said in a pleasant English tone.

I bowed politely over her hand as Katy giggled.

"You must forgive Katy, Charles. The conventions of polite society are foreign to her," Emma scolded.

"Don't bother much with that stuff here," said another man in a harsh Texas rasp. "I'm Jerry Dodge, Chuck. Nice to meetcha. I'm the wrangler for this place."

"Katy tells me that you're going to be working here for a couple of weeks. What are you going to be doing?" Emma asked.

Katy intercepted the question again for me.

"The Queen wants him to spend time everywhere, and she asked us all to help shape him up."

She reached for my tray.

"In fact, I'll start right now." She took the piece of pie I has taken and proceeded to hit me in the face with it. "You are on a diet. Remember?"

I sat with the cream dripping from my face. There were far more polite ways to remind me of that fact, and most of them less embarrassing. I wanted to say something, but I couldn't. I did, however, reach for the pie on Jerry Dodge's tray.

"You wouldn't dare!" she said as I picked it up.

I hefted it, measuring the distance and considering the results, and glared at her. The rest of the group sat waiting for the strike. I didn't want an incident, but I didn't relish letting the insult go unpunished.

I gently set the pie slice down on Jerry's tray and wiped the remnants of my slice from my face. Wordlessly, I pantomimed bending her over my lap and spanking her.

The whole group broke out in laughter, and Emma tossed me a napkin.

"You guys sure take your vows seriously," Jerry laughed. "I mean turn the other cheek and all. I'd a hit her."

"He just knows how to control himself better than you do," Katy said. "Don't you?"

I nodded. She was of Ay'esha. I knew that now from her speech habits. In a natural motion, I touched the medallion around my neck as she nodded in acknowledgment.

"Finish up, Charles. The Queen wants to see you after dinner," she said.

I ate my dinner in reasonable silence and was escorted to an office on the second floor of the building.

The Queen sat behind a large desk waiting for me. I knelt before her upon entering and heard Katy close the door behind me.

"Well I see you know what to do in my presence. I was watching that little incident in the dining room on the monitor camera. You did very well. Katy was under orders to try and break your silence. Katy and I are the only ones here who know exactly who you are. To the rest of them you are Charles Freeman. You have been sent here to survey our operations. You will tell them nothing else. You will follow the training program laid out for you. You will keep your conversations with the guests to a minimum."

The Queen got up and walked to my side of the desk.

"You will obey any orders that Katy gives you, as if they were mine. Understood?"

I nodded in agreement.

"When you leave here you may speak again. Go!" she commanded and directed me towards the door.

I exited and found Katy waiting for me.

She took me by the arm and led me outside onto a balcony overlooking the sea.

"Would spanking me make you feel any better?" she teased.

"No, Miss," I said, looking into the night sky.

"It's Katy, not Miss. I have no title. Not Mistress, Master, or anything else. I still need to earn one. Perhaps, you can help."

"What kind of help could I provide?"

"If you tried to escape, I could stop you. That way, the Queen might be impressed enough to give me a title."

"No."

"No, what?" she pressed.

"Miss Katy, I'm not going to escape or even have it look as if I were trying to escape. I don't want to escape."

"Why?"

"Because, I love my Mistress. I will not risk my returning to her to help you. You will earn your title as I have earned mine. By working hard," I told her.

She scoffed at that.

"What possible title could you own. After all, you're just a slave."

"I am Mistress Minx's slave. I could ask for no better title than that," I replied proudly.

A gleam came into her eye. "You have been instructed to follow my orders as well as the Queen's. Right?"

"Yes, Miss Katy."

"Then, follow me, slave"

XX

Katy escorted me back to my room and locked me in. She returned a few minutes later with a canvas travel bag and locked the door behind her.

"Now slave, let's play. Strip!"

I removed my clothes and knelt at her feet and waited.

With quick hands she tied my hands and feet behind me and stepped back to assess her handiwork.

"Now, slave, do you know what I enjoy doing?"

I shook my head.

She reached into her bag and removed a wig and a makeup case.

"I enjoy making little boys into little girls. It gets me very hot."

I recoiled at the thought somewhat. I'm not a real good looking man, but as a woman? I tried to back away from her, but the second she detected movement she grabbed me by my hair and stopped me.

"Naughty boy! Momma will spank you, if you don't hold still for her."

I continued my resistance until she collared me with one hand and attached it to the bed frame.

"Now that I have your attention, I will start with lipstick. A nice bright red shade should suit you."

The pain of her grip on my hair was rapidly overcoming my objections to the procedure, so I relaxed to the inevitable. I felt like a dog a little girl was playing dress up with.

She painted my lips with precision, despite my flinching from her touch. The next step was makeup to cover my less than female skin texture. It seemed like hours before she finished and proceeded to put the wig on me.

"Now, little girl. Let's see the results!"

She untied me, released the collar from the bed and marched me into the bathroom. Reflected in the mirror was, well, sure not what I expected to see. I actually didn't look half bad, as compared with all bad.

"You make a very nice girl. Next time, I'll dress you up as the slut you are," she crowed.

I could feel myself blushing under the makeup at that idea. It seemed to arouse me, as well.

She led me back to the bed and pushed me down onto it and straddled my chest, while she tied my hands to the bed. She leaned back with a smile on her face and removed her shirt to reveal a lovely firm pair of tits. I saw for the first time she had pierced nipples, with small silver rings inserted.

"Would you like to suck my tits, little girl?" she asked, toying with her nipples.

"Oh yes," I whispered, fascinated by the light reflecting off the rings.

"Tell your Mommy what you want, little girl," she crooned.

"Please, Mommy, let me suck your tits. I'm so hungry," I whimpered like a tired child.

She brushed her nipples across my red painted lips as I opened my mouth. She teased me with them, keeping them just out of range of my eager mouth. Then, she plunged her left tit in my mouth and commanded me to suck. I could taste the metal of the ring and the cherry flavor of the lipstick combined with sweet woman flesh. I relaxed into submission with my face buried in her breasts, licking and sucking as she directed.

I could feel a slight dampness on my chest and smell her musk as she became even more aroused.

She raped my mouth with her tongue, smearing lipstick all over her face and mine. My cock became hard, as she thrust her tongue deeper each time. She slid back and trapped my cock under her, rubbing it against her now damp shorts.

"I want you to cum!" she demanded, removing her shorts and rubbing her now exposed pussy against my prick.

I moaned from the sensations. I wanted to cum, but I couldn't let myself. Katy was demanding something I had no right to give her. Mistress Minx owned my seed, not I.

Then, it was too late. I exploded all over Katy's belly and tits. She collected the cum from her belly with her fingers and shoved it into my mouth.

"Eat it, little girl. I want you to eat your cum. I'm going to teach you to eat another man's cum before you leave here," she hissed, as I sucked the filth from her fingers.

She rolled off me and dressed again. Before she left me bound for the night, she removed the wig and stuffed it into her bag.

"I will be back at six to wake you up," she said unlocking the door. "And I might have a treat for you, if you're a good girl."

She switched off the light and left, leaving me painted and cum-soaked until morning.

XXI

Morning came all too early for me after the activity of the night before. My reverie was broken by the sound of the lock clicking and Katy coming in dressed in a jogging suit and carrying another one.

"Good morning," she said smiling down at my bound form. "After you shower, we're going jogging before breakfast."

"How delightful," I replied sarcastically. "And, what other affronts do you bring to my day?"

She untied my hands from the bed and stood up. "My, my little girl is cranky this morning. Perhaps she needs a spanking to change her mood."

I rolled out of bed and headed for the shower with Katy trailing behind me.

A few minutes of hot water and I felt somewhat more normal, and even ashamed of being cranky. My mood brightened even more when I was joined by a slippery wet Katy who insisted on helping to scrub my back and remove the makeup from the night before.

She treated me as a partner, rather than as a slave. It was still a bit uncommon to be treated that way, but I reminded myself that she had her own ways of controlling a man.

She helped dry me off, and I dressed in the jogging suit. It actually fit, which explained the reasons for the measurements Mrs. Queen had taken. A pair of shoes in my size completed the outfit, and I followed Katy down the hall and outside towards the beach.

I will say it was a nice change to be jogging on a beach, rather than on a treadmill in a lab, wired to a set of electrodes designed to shock me, if I slowed down.

It wasn't all pleasure, though, for as I reached the end of the course that Katy had indicated, she stopped me and climbed on my back to be carried the rest of the way back to the main house.

She couldn't have weighed much more than a hundred pounds, but jogging in sand with a hundred pounds of extra mass really weighs on the knees. I made it, though, but at a considerably reduced pace from the outbound trip.

"That was pretty good for a first time. Tomorrow you can carry me both ways, and we'll see what happens to your time," she said as I set her down and collapsed on the sand.

"You do have a mean streak, don't you?" I said, gasping for breath.

"Yes. Remember it, slave. The Queen wants you trained in certain ways, and it's my job to see you trained. Besides it's what I do anyway."

"What do you mean by that?" I said, sitting up.

"Didn't I tell you what my job here is? I'm in charge of physical training for the Spa. And, some of the women are in worse shape than you are. If I can whip them into shape, I can literally do the same to you. Now get up and follow me. I want you to spend some time in the gym before you eat."

I got to my feet and followed my new taskmistress to the gym.

From my point of view, all of the exercise machines looked like torture devices after that jog, but I cooperated and placed myself in a machine designed to build up my stomach muscles. Actually it was designed to force me to do sit-ups at a rate that no sane person would do them.

"Now I'm setting this to slow, so you can adjust to it. It's probably going to hurt for a bit until you get used to it. I'll only set it for five minutes this time, but before you leave, you'll do it twenty minutes at a time."

"Willingly?" I asked suspiciously.

Her voice hardened slightly. "Or, not. Your choice, slave. Now, be quiet. I'm going to pick out your breakfast for you today, because I can't trust you to stay on your diet. I'll be back in a few minutes."

With that, she started the machine and left.

The person who designed the machine obviously was a student of the Inquisition. I was bent and unbent repeatedly for five long minutes. The machine sighed to a stop, and I sat up.

I had noticed a set of fencing foils in a corner of the gym, so I decided to try them out. Now, I'm no expert with a sword, but I had taken Kendo at one time.

I had just put on the fencing mask and picked up the foil when another woman entered the gym.

"Good morning," I offered. "I was just fooling around a bit."

"I didn't think anybody else would be in here at this time," she said walking towards me.

"If I had a choice, I wouldn't be here myself," I said pulling off the mask. "I'm Charles Freeman."

"Are you employed here, Mr. Freeman?"

Without the mask on, I could see her clearly. She was about my height, middle-aged, and dark-haired with a strong German accent.

"Not exactly. I'm just checking things out. I'll be working in various places, as well as taking advantage of the facilities here to shape up a bit," I said, reciting my cover story.

She picked up a mask and foil and offered to teach me a lesson.

"I wouldn't mind some instruction. I've never used a foil before."

She placed the mask on as did I and moved to the center of the fencing area. "En garde!"

I knew what that meant, at least. I tried to remember all of the swashbuckler movies I had seen, but all I could think of was *The Court Jester* with Danny Kaye, who couldn't handle a sword at all.

We crossed blades with the singing sound of steel. I parried as well as I could as she pressed her attack, then got mad and started really fighting back. She was more skillful, but I was more intent on winning.

The battle royale was broken by Katy's return with my breakfast.

"What are you two doing?" she interrupted sharply.

The sound of her voice proved my undoing as my mystery

adversary slipped under my guard to pierce my jogging suit over my heart.

"Touché."

I removed the mask and bowed to my enemy, who was unmasking, as well.

"You fought well for someone with no training. You would make a good student," she complimented me warmly.

"Well, if I catch either of you fighting without a vest again, I will make sure that Mrs. Queen hears about it. You know the rules, Mrs. Hoffmann," Katy scolded us.

"Katy, it's my fault. I was just fooling around, and Mrs. Hoffmann, is it, offered to teach me," I assured her.

"Mrs. Hoffmann is our fencing instructor, Charles. You're very lucky she is as skilled as she is. You could have been hurt."

"I'm just fine. Tired, though. You know, I never realized how much work fencing is." Katy started to regain her composure after her outburst and suggested that perhaps fencing could be added to my training routine.

"I would be happy to train him. Perhaps after normal hours," agreed Mrs. Hoffmann.

"Well, I'll let the two of you determine my fate. Katy, you know my schedule. If you can work fencing into my stay here, I would appreciate it. I'm sure Mrs. Queen would agree," I said, turning towards my rapidly cooling breakfast on a nearby table.

I was rewarded with a somewhat poisonous look from Katy, as I turned away.

When she completed her negotiations, Katy returned to my side in less than a good mood. "What sort of fool are you?"

"Oh, just your everyday fool, I guess," I said lightly.

"You could have been hurt. And it would be my fault," she continued.

I picked up a piece of dry toast and dunked it into my coffee and looked at her.

"I could have been hurt last night, too. But, I wasn't. Did you tell the Queen about last night?"

She sort of hemmed and hawed and admitted she hadn't.

"Why, not? She does have the right to know. Or, perhaps you don't think she would approve of last nights recreation?" I suggested.

"Probably, not. I was afraid you might get into trouble."

I looked at her and smiled. "Katy, if I get into trouble, I have it coming. I was told to follow your orders, and that you had full authority over me. If anything, you'd be the one in trouble, for letting me get into trouble."

She looked at me with a strange expression. "I don't understand you."

I pointed to my head. "Never mind. Why do you think I have gray hairs? That way I can worry and nobody can tell. What's my first class today, anyway? Hopefully, something not too strenuous."

"As a matter of fact, you should enjoy it. You're going to learn how to give a proper foot massage today. So, let's get you showered again and into your new clothes," she instructed.

"What new clothes?" I asked, suspecting the worst.

"Well, if you're going to work here, you have to dress like the rest of the staff. And, I know maroon is just your color. You'll love it."

XXII

I hated it. I was now dressed in a maroon smock and matching pants. I don't mind a little private humiliation, but this was going to be all too public.

"I think you look cute," Katy commented. "But, you'll look better when I put you in a corset and heels.

I sneered at her. "Thank you. I'll be sure to remember that. It might be useful under a bizarre set of circumstances."

She led me out of my room and into the foyer of the house. It was the first time I had been in the main part of the house. Up to that point, Katy had kept me out of the main public areas. I was more than impressed with the décor. In fact, if I'd had a choice, I would have never gone into a place like this.

I froze for a moment at the doorway and looked around.

"What's wrong?" Katy asked. "Did you see someone?"

"No, it just that...well, I'm not used to a place like this. I'm a pretty common sort of guy."

She smiled in reassurance. "Common is not how I would describe you. Now, remember who you are."

"Who I am?"

"You are Mistress Minx's slave. Definitely, a cut above the common," she reminded me.

Mistress Minx's slave. Deep breath. "Lead on, Miss Katy."

She led me across the vast lobby to the main desk and introduced me to the head clerk.

"Mr. Freeman will be working here for the time being. Show him how you want things done."

The head clerk sniffed disdainfully at me and asked if I'd had any resort experience at all.

"No, sir. I'm afraid not," I apologized.

He looked at Katy.

"Is he another one of Mrs. Queen's pets, Miss Katherine?" he asked sourly.

"Yes, Mr. Terwilliger."

His eyes rolled back in his head. "I hope he's more competent than the last one. Well, we'll see what happens."

I listened carefully as he outlined what he expected of me. I would be assisting him at the desk to start with as a bellboy.

I wasn't the best bellboy he'd ever had, but he did concede I was far from the worst. I learned how to pack things properly, how to unpack a bag and lay things out, and how to avoid problems with women who wanted to make more intimate use of me.

That was only part of my day.

I studied with a massage therapist and learned how to give a proper massage. I worked in the salon and learned how to do a pedicure and a manicure. I studied chemistry and learned how to mix hair dyes and solutions properly.

Some of my previous experience with superglue came in handy when one of the other people accidentally glued himself to a client. Nail polish remover took it right off.

Mr. Terwilliger had me do some of the bookkeeping and in fact my computer skills even saved the Spa some money.

My morning jog with Katy was still a pain, although I was getting a bit better at carrying her. She just kept increasing the distance and time.

"Are you trying to get me in shape to run a marathon?" I asked after we finished one day.

"And, why not? You're in pretty good shape for a man your age," she said flatly.

The tone of her voice hurt me slightly. A man of my age. "You are my physical trainer, Miss Katy. And my Mistress by proxy. Am I failing to perform or serve properly?"

"You are doing very well. Better in some ways than I had expected. Your body is becoming better fit everyday. The reports I have from Emma on your self defense training show a latent ability. And, the fencing lessons from Mrs. Hoffmann aren't hurting you, either."

"Thank you, Miss Katy."

"But, you are not spending enough time serving women. I'm going to have you moved to the salon and the kitchen."

I tried to control my nervousness. Up to that point, I had pretty well managed to stay in the background unnoticed.

"Yes, Miss Katy. When do you want me to start?"

"This afternoon. This morning, I want you to take me to town."

I wasn't sure if I had heard her correctly. "Excuse me, Miss Katy? You want me to take you off the grounds?"

"Yes, I need to pick up some people in town, and the other drivers aren't available. You do drive, don't you?"

"Yes, but I'm not sure I should leave the grounds."

"I am in charge of you. You weren't planning on running away were you?"

"No, Miss Katy."

"Good. Get changed and meet me in the lobby in ten minutes."

I did as I was told, although I was still a bit nervous about it. Once I was off the grounds I could escape if I wanted to. The idea of freedom again tempted me. But, freedom to do what? To return to my old life, my old habits?

But I could go home again. My house, my bed. My books and comforts. But did they still exist? What had happened to my things while I was gone?

At what a price! I would lose Mistress Minx.

The second night at the spa, I had picked up the telephone in my room. It worked. I was tempted to call someone. Anyone, just to hear a voice that was not under the control of Ay'esha.
I put the phone back down carefully.

Who could I call? And again, the question of why?

When Katy and I reached the gatepost, the guard just looked at us and waved us through.

I drove down the highway as Katy chattered away about things happening at the Spa that I was too busy to notice. It was a nice day and listening to Katy I felt alive and aware of the world after my isolation.

She directed me to the small airport and ordered me to stop in front of the main terminal.

I got out and helped load the bags into the van as Katy introduced me to the new guests.

"Charles, this is Janice. She's a very old friend of mine," Katy said and I bowed in respect.

Janice was a large woman with her hair in a bun that gave her a motherly presence.

"Well, he's sure trained well, Katy. Is he one of your boys?" Janice asked smiling at me.

"No, he's just well mannered," Katy denied.

"That's not quite true, Miss Janice. She's the one that's keeping me in line. Otherwise I'd be a real pain in the ass." I said without thinking.

Katy looked at me in shock, and I started to apologize for my language when it was cut off by Janice's laughter.

"I like him. He's not afraid to speak up."

The woman standing behind her, however, had a little different take. "Impertinent is what I would call it," she said with a chill in her voice that would have frozen a polar bear.

She was dark haired, thin, but muscular, and wore a business suit.

"Charles, this is Ms. Claire," Katy said quickly.

Ms. Claire thrust the briefcase in her hand to me and ordered me to store it carefully. "I expect you will curb your tongue when in my presence. I expect you to respond quickly to my orders and keep your mouth shut otherwise."

I nodded quickly.

A young blond woman introduced herself to Katy as Amanda Gayle. "This is my first time here. I read the ads and had to see for myself."

"I hope you enjoy yourself. We have many activities for your enjoyment. Horseback riding, swimming, a full gym and spa," Katy said warmly.

Amanda looked at me and smiled at Katy.

"I'm sure I will. Would you get my bags, please, Charles?" she asked.

I picked them up and almost fell over from the weight. It took two hands to get them up, and I almost pulled my shoulder out placing them in the van.

"Excuse me, Miss Amanda. Do you mind telling me what you have in your bags?" I asked.

"Books. I'm an author and a reviewer. I need some time away from my office to catch up, so I brought them with me," she said.

Our last passenger was a young Asian woman who introduced herself as Judy Chen. "My company thought I needed a rest, so they sent me here," she said shaking hands with Katy," I think they need a rest from me."

I liked her easy way of talking. She wore glasses and had a cheerful expression.

With everything loaded in the van, I drove us back to the Spa and unloaded everything as Katy helped the ladies register.

Mr. Terwilliger came out a few moments later and directed me to take the bags to their rooms. This time, I had the sense to get a cart to move Miss Amanda's books to her room.

Ms. Claire accepted the briefcase from me, directed me to place her other bags in the closet and told me to get out.

I did so, gratefully.

Miss Janice patted me on the ass, as I unpacked her things as she directed.

"Nice ass," she said.

"Thank you. I like it," I said with a smile.

"I like an honest slave."

I feigned confusion at her words.

"Slave? I'm sorry I don't understand."

She grinned at me and from between her breasts removed a medallion identical to mine.

"Of course, you don't."

I knelt before her without comment.

"You are a good slave. How long have you been here?"

"A short time. Mistress Minx sent me here for training."

Mistress Janice, looked impressed. "You are a slave to Mistress Minx?"

"Yes, Mistress."

"You are very special indeed. You may go now," she directed.

Miss Judy just had me place the bags inside the room and leave.

I reported back to Mr. Terwilliger for another assignment and was told to report to the kitchen.

"Miss Katy is interested in seeing what kind of a waiter you'll make. Myself, I'm interested in seeing what sort of a mess you'll make," he said.

"Your confidence is overwhelming."

"Young man, you remind me of my students. A miserable bunch."

"Students? What did you teach?" I asked.

"Piano. The little wretches simply would not practice as I had directed. I finally had enough and retired from teaching."

"Well, if you showed the same amount of confidence in them as you do me, I understand the problem."

He glared at me as I left for the kitchen, and I didn't care.

The headwaiter gave me a quick rundown on my duties and sent me to work.

Everything was just fine until Ms. Claire came in for lunch.

Nothing was right for her. The soup was too cold, the salad was wilted, and the steak was undercooked. With each new complaint my sense of humor shrank as well as that of the chef.

He finally managed to prepare it just the way she wanted it. Of course, the urge to add a little rat poison was there, too.

The rest of the day went along with a minimum of errors. Not that I didn't make a few, but the people involved understood it was my first day as a waiter.

By the time I got off work and headed to my room to change for my fencing lesson, I was ready to kill something.

My aggression was noted by Mrs. Hoffmann. "Your thrusts are

very powerful tonight, Charles, but your focus is elsewhere," she said after a few minutes of practice. "Would you like to skip the lesson this evening?"

I apologized for my lack of focus, but that didn't satisfy her.

"If you are angry and upset, it would be useless to practice. Is there anything I can do?" she asked.

"No, Ma'am. One of the new guests is a bit difficult. And she and I don't seem to get along very well."

"Would I be in error if I suggested that the party in question is Ms. Claire?" she said, hanging her fencing foil on a hook.

"No, you would not," I said removing my fencing mask.

"She isn't an easy person to get along with. Especially, if you are male. She'd rather see you shot after being castrated."

Sounded like a friend of Lydia for sure.

"Well, I'll try and avoid her. Thanks for the warning," I said.

"Certainly. Why don't you go over to the sauna for awhile? I'll send Katy over there and tell her your lesson was canceled," she suggested.

I thought about it for a moment and agreed.

The sauna area was empty, but I didn't want to take any chances, so I made sure I posted the OCCUPIED sign on the room I was in. I stretched out in the hot room and tried to relax.

My mind kept going back to the Mother of Many's warning, as she placed the medallion around my neck.

"To those who know, this medallion indicates you are owned and part of Ay'esha. Until now, no member would harm you while you wore this. With Lydia's departure from our ranks, I would caution you to be wary of those you do not know, be they male or female."

I fell asleep finally and woke up a short time later sweating profusely. I rolled off the bench and opened the door. Or I should say tried to open the door. It wouldn't move. I thought it might have swollen shut, so I pushed a little harder. Nothing. I looked out the small porthole in the door and saw that someone had placed a stack of weights from the gym in front of the door, blocking it closed.

I looked towards the thermometer on the wall and saw the temperature was rising slowly towards the danger zone. I tried to turn the heat down with the controls on the wall but the needle kept rising.

I started to panic. Someone was trying to cook me alive. I threw myself at the door and thought I felt it move slightly. I tried again and again. Nothing. I didn't have enough weight to force the door open.

I lay back down on the bench and thought as the heat increased. I didn't have anything to break the porthole with, did I? Yes I did. My fist. I wrapped my hand in the towel I had been wearing and faced the door.

Remember the power flows through the arm and into the fist. I remembered what Emma had told me as I focused on the porthole.

Through the fist. I punched the porthole and was rewarded by a sharp pain in my hand and a crack in the glass.

Once more. The fist struck the glass and the crack widened.

I changed fists and tried one more time.

The glass shattered, and I felt cooler air flow into the sauna and gulped it eagerly.

Both my hands were swollen from the punches, and I was sure I'd broken at least one finger.

I started yelling for help through the porthole and was rewarded by Jerry Dodge running into the room and pulling the weights away from the door.

"What the hell happened?" he asked, pulling me from the sauna.

I turned to look back and saw my OCCUPIED sign had been changed to an OUT OF ORDER sign.

"I was relaxing and fell asleep. I guess someone was moving equipment and parked it there without seeing the OCCUPIED sign I put up," I said toweling off.

"That sign says OUT OF ORDER," Jerry said.

"Well I put up an OCCUPIED sign. Guess the person who parked the weights must have changed it."

"Man, you could have been killed," he said.

"Don't I know it."

Later, back in my room, I thought about the incident. I knew it was no accident that the weights had been left there. The question was who did it? Mrs. Hoffmann knew I was going to the sauna. And she had said she would tell Katy where I was. But anybody could have seen me sleeping in there and taken advantage of it.

And where was Katy? She never had shown up, and when I went to her room, she wasn't there.

Should I tell the Queen about the incident? Who could I trust?

Lyrics from a forgotten song intruded into my thoughts. "Paranoia runs deep, into your life it will creep."

Now, I really understood it.

I locked the door that night for the first time and tried to sleep.

I woke up to the sound of a key turning in the lock and rolled over to look towards the door.

Katy crept into the room and crawled into the bed with me, as I sat up and turned on the light.

She blinked and apologized for waking me.

"Miss Katy, where have you been?" I asked softly.

"Didn't you get my note? The Queen wanted me to go into town again for supplies. I left you a note about it."

"I never got it," I said, looking her in the eye.

"I slipped it under the door."

She rolled out of bed and handed me a piece of paper lying next to the door.

I read it and tossed it aside. "Sorry. I guess I missed it when I came in earlier. I was in a pretty bad mood."

"Well, I'm here now. What's wrong?" she asked innocently.

"Nothing. Just a hard day with Ms. Claire."

"She is a bitch, isn't she?" she giggled. "I wanted to slap her when she was so rude to you."

"I think Rudolfo wanted to poison her after her comments about his cooking," I said with a snicker of my own.

Katy crawled back into bed and snuggled next to me. "Don't worry about it. Just do your best."

I kissed her softly and was rewarded by a slap for my efforts.

"Naughty boy. I'll kiss you when I choose to," she reminded me.

"Yes, Mistress."

"Stop that," she said, as the lights went out.

The next thing I remembered was being awakened by my

exercise coach.

After my run with Katy on the beach, she suggested we take a swim in the pool before breakfast instead of my time in the gym.

"Miss Katy, I don't swim very well," I warned.

"That's okay. Neils will save you," she said and ran laughing towards the pool.

She dove into it like a seal, while I followed more like a walrus.

Neils was already in his chair watching the pool even at that early hour.

"Neils, do you ever leave that chair?" I called from the pool.

"Only to sleep and eat. I'm here from the time the pool opens to the time it closes. Safety first," he replied.

"Do you give the swimming lessons, too?"

"Yes, and the scuba lessons as well. Katy assists me for those classes."

I looked at Katy who was floating in the deep end of the pool.

"Is there anything else I should know about you?" I called.

She splashed water towards me, dove for the bottom, and before I could defend myself, pulled off my shorts.

"Katy!" I said, as she waved them in the air.

"If you want them, you have to catch me!" she said and headed for the deep end again.

As I pondered my ability to catch her without drowning, Miss Judy and Miss Amanda arrived.

"Well, I see this place has everything. Even naked pool boys!" Miss Amanda laughed upon seeing my shorts being held by Katy.

"Come on, Katy, this isn't funny any more," I called hotly.

"Be nice to me, Charles. Or, I'll throw them in the drain," she said.

Neils finally decided to take a hand in matters at that point by diving in and pulling Katy to the bottom.

She released my shorts, and they floated to the surface, where Miss Judy dived in and recovered them.

"Here you are," she said tossing them to me.

I slipped into them as Katy and Neils rose to the surface again.

"I'll get you for that, Neils!" she said, coughing.

"You need to remember how to escape from a drowning person, Katy. Practice makes perfect," he said, climbing out of the pool and sitting back down in his tower.

I thanked Miss Judy, climbed out of the water and followed Katy towards the main house.

"Why didn't you come after me?" she said with a hint of anger.

"Miss Katy, I can't swim very well. I almost drowned as a child, and I've been a bit afraid of water ever since," I admitted.

"I'm sorry. I wouldn't have done that if I'd known," she said, mollified.

To make up for it, Katy brought me my breakfast, and I had just started eating when Jerry came in.

"Boy, you really made a mess last night," he said clapping me on the shoulder.

I shook my head to warn him, off but it was too late.

"What happened?" Katy said looking at me.

"Aw, hell. Some idiot locked him in the sauna. He had to break the window to get someone's attention. It's a good thing I was there. He coulda been cooked."

Katy looked at me narrowly. "So, nothing happened last night?"

I gulped.

"We need to see the Queen about this after breakfast," she said.

I didn't feel much like eating after that, but what the hell?

The interview with the Queen was short and to the point.

"I am responsible for your safety while you are in training here. Any more incidents like this need to be reported to me or Katy at once!" she said.

"Ma'am, yes, ma'am!" I snapped from my kneeling position.

"Katy, take him out and punish him. I'll let you decide what sort of punishment to administer," she directed.

Katy ordered me to crawl out on my hands and knees. She sat in a chair in the outer office, while I knelt at her feet.

"Well, what can I do to you? Something that will always remind you to tell the truth to me," she said thinking aloud.

I just waited for her. I had it coming, and I knew it. Even though I had been warned not to trust anyone, I couldn't tell her that.

"I have a perfect punishment in mind for you," she finally said. "Come with me, slave!"

A few minutes later I was dressed in my jogging suit and being strapped into the exercise machine that forced me to do sit ups.

"Now, you are going to suffer. I'm going to set the machine for the maximum number of cycles and watch. By the time I'm finished with you, you will tell me anything I want to know," Katy said pulling the last strap tight.

"Mistress, please," I begged.

"No. You have to be punished for lying." She started the machine and stepped back.

I was bent forward then back, over and over again. Each cycle bent me like a pretzel and the sweat poured off of me along with the tears of pain.

"You will not hide anything from me again. You will tell me anything I want to know," she said as the machine tore at me.

"Yes, Mistress," I sobbed through the pain.

To add to my embarrassment, Ms. Claire entered the gym, watched me being twisted and laughed.

"Much better. That should keep the little swine in line," she said.

Over and over again I was bent. My back and stomach muscles rebelled and I vomited my breakfast onto myself.

This was worse than being beaten. The machine never stopped or slowed or took a break. It just tortured me. No feeling, no mercy, no pleasure. Simply a mechanical action.

My vision started blurring from the exertion, and then became a gray fog.

The machine sighed to a stop at last, and I lay back limply in the seat covered in sweat and vomit.

"Now he should eat his vomit," Ms. Claire commented savagely.

I lay there, eyes closed and waited for Katy's order.

I would do anything she wanted to be released from the clutches of the machine.

"I don't think so," said Katy. "But, he is going to clean it up. With his hands."

I felt her release the straps and as the last one was released, I fell limply to the floor.

"Now clean up the mess you made and thank me for permitting you to use your hands instead of your mouth," Katy snapped.

I opened my eyes to see the remnants of my meal and then looked at her with tears in my eyes.

"Thank you, Mistress, for letting me clean up my mess," I said weakly.

She grabbed my hair and pulled my head back. "Louder!"

"Thank you, Mistress, for letting me clean up my mess!" I said in a louder tone.

She released her grip, and I slowly gathered the mess into a pile on the floor and removed my shirt to swab it up.

"Tell me, Katy, haven't you ever really wanted to hurt one of these little swine until he screamed?" Ms. Claire asked her, as I mopped up the slime.

"No, I really enjoy making them suffer silently. I don't want to hear them at all," Katy said.

"With an attitude like that, I can see why you aren't a real Mistress yet. Lydia would never approve of someone as soft as you are on men."

Lydia. Even in my weakened state I felt a surge of fear.

"Perhaps you're right. But I'd rather torture a real man, rather than a man like this," Katy replied.

I just lay there, head on the floor waiting for permission to move or speak.

I heard Ms. Claire walk away and waited for the next phase of my punishment.

"Are you all right?" Katy whispered in my ear.

"No, Mistress. I hurt," I moaned.

"Good. Will you obey me now?" she asked.

"Yes, Mistress."

She half dragged and half carried me to a bench and lay me

down on my back.

"I'm going to get you a drink. Just stay there."

I did as I was commanded and didn't move. Even the thought of a friend of Lydia's wasn't enough to cause me to budge.

Katy returned with a squeeze bottle of water and let me suck on it slowly, saying nothing, just looking down at me. "I want to know why someone would be interested in hurting you." I hesitated for a moment. I had promised to obey, but if she was in league with Lydia, it was just as likely I would be put back on the machine and left until I was dead.

"Mistress, I can't tell you. The Mother of Many told me not to," I said plaintively.

Katy looked at me intensely. "You know the Mother of Many?"

"Yes, Mistress. She gave me my medallion."

"I will not ask you to violate your promise to the Mother of Many. But, if there is danger to any one else around you, I must know."

She was right. I had been warned not to trust people, but I couldn't let someone be hurt because of my silence. "Do you know Lydia?"

"I've heard about her. She doesn't care much for men at all. I guess that's why Claire likes her."

"Lydia has left Ay'esha. She disagreed with the Mother of Many and left with some others."

Katy looked at me in disbelief. "But, why? It makes no sense. She would have been the Mother of Many eventually."

"She and Mistress Minx disagreed about me. My Mistress feels that men can be trained to serve willingly without brutality. I offered myself for punishment to spare Mistress Minx for an error I made, and Lydia thought I was a fool. She claimed that my willingness to suffer in place of my Mistress proved that men were unworthy to survive without being under control."

"And were you punished?"

I took a deep breath and another drink of water. "Yes. And Minx whipped me herself. It was her right as my Mistress to punish me. She was going to be punished for my mistake, and I couldn't let her do it," I said quietly.

"But, as a slave you are an animal. If you make an error, you are not responsible for it," Katy objected.

"And that is why Lydia left Ay'esha. I insisted on taking responsibility for my actions even when I didn't have to. I refused to be a dumb animal when it meant pain for my Mistress. I love Mistress Minx with all my heart."

XXIII

Katy sat silently, considering my words. "What would happen, if Lydia had found you?"

I looked her in the eye. "I would be killed by her."

"You're not serious."

"She is. You didn't see the expression on her face. She really does want to kill me. And, I don't want to die at her hands," I said, trembling at the memory of her words:

"And you, slave. There will come a time when you will regret this meeting. I shall not kill or harm a sister, but you will pay for your foolish ways."

Katy touched me softly. "You mean it. She would kill you."

"Like you might swat a fly," I said.

She shook her head. "Not here. I won't let it."

"You can't watch me all the time Mistress," I said quietly.

"When you are not working or in class, you will stay in your room with the door locked," she ordered.

"Yes, Mistress. But, I don't think it will help," I said docilely.

"At least whoever tried will have a harder time," she observed.

"Or, an easier one. If I'm always in one place, I'm a sitting duck."

She sighed. "Do you always argue with your Mistress?"

"No, Mistress, I'm sorry, Mistress," I said cringing at the rebuke.

She patted me on the head and tugged me by my chain. "Come

along."

The Queen was less than amused, but agreed with Katy that the possibility of an innocent bystander being hit outweighed the security aspects.

"Steps will have to be taken to increase security. Make sure he does not roam after dark without an escort," the Queen instructed. "The rest of the time there are enough people around to make an incident unlikely."

"What about at night?" Katy asked.

The Queen's lips formed a small smile. "I believe your current sleeping arrangements will provide enough security for him."

I blushed, and Katy didn't.

"I know everything that goes on in this house. Never doubt it," the Queen warned. I didn't doubt that for a moment.

Katy led me back to my room and pushed me into the shower to get me cleaned up from the earlier activities.

When I stepped out she threw my work clothes at me and ordered me to report to the kitchen.

"Back to work for you, slave. When you finish, I will meet you here. You will not go to the gym or anyplace outside of this building after dark without an escort or telling me."

"Yes, Mistress," I said getting dressed hastily. The tone of her voice conveyed her annoyance and dissatisfaction with the Queen's decision.

"And stop calling me 'Mistress.' If you have to call me anything formally, stick to Miss Katy."

"Yes, Miss Katy. Please, don't worry."

"I want you to leave here. It's not worth your life," she said.

I reached out and touched her arm gently. "I have nothing else to do. I don't have a home, a job or anything else, Miss Katy. I've been a prisoner for, well, I'm not really sure how long. My friends probably think I'm dead. So what do I have to go to? At least here I have something like a home and people who do care about me."

"I'm sorry," she said.

I took a deep breath. "I'm not. I was much worse off before. At least I know someone loves me now. I had forgotten that I could be loved."

She kissed me softly on the cheek. "Never forget that."

Even though I felt like I needed eyes in the back of my head, I actually avoided making any errors than day as a waiter. In fact, the only unpleasant moment came from Miss Claire who asked if I had enjoyed my exercise earlier.

"Yes, Miss Claire. Thank you for asking," I said without a trace of sarcasm.

Rudolfo spent some time during the lull between lunch and dinner showing me how to make a plate attractive. It really is an art form to place the parsley sprig just so and to cut the tomato so it forms a rose. I'd never really appreciated that fact until I watched a master chef do it.

"Now paisano, you try one. Make a rose for me," he said, handing me a knife and a ripe tomato.

Eight tomatoes later he stopped me.

"Well, now I don't have to chop tomatoes for the sauces tonight," he laughed. "Practice makes perfect. You can practice a little every day until you get it right."

He swept the remains of my efforts into a pot and wiped his hands.

"Well, I guess I'm not very good with a knife," I apologized.

"Ah, but you are with a sword. Mrs. Hoffmann was commenting on how good you are," he said.

"She hasn't said anything to me about it. I guess she doesn't want my head to swell," I replied.

He chuckled. "I wouldn't worry. She'd just pop it like a balloon."

Now that was a scary thought.

The dinner service that night was light, and at one of my tables was Janice and Amanda. They both ordered the steak and shrimp dinner, and I felt privileged to be able to help Rudolfo make it look good.

I delivered the meal with a flourish and a polite bow and asked if there were anything else I could bring them.

Janice just looked at me and smiled. "Yes. Feed me my shrimp with your fingers."

I was a bit uncertain of what I should do, so I decided that an order was an order. I took the first shrimp and dipped it into the sauce as directed, and she nibbled her way up to my fingers as Amanda watched in a mixture of amazement and amusement.

"Would you like him to feed you, too?" Janice asked her.

Amanda looked at me with interest and nodded.

I spent the next ten minutes feeding the two women their shrimp before being released to return to my regular work.

Saul, the headwaiter, looked at me aghast as I went back into the kitchen, and I waited for his wrath to descend upon me.

"Would you like to tell me exactly what you were doing with those two ladies?"

"I was feeding shrimp to them, sir," I said honestly.

"You were feeding them shrimp," he mimicked. "And while you were feeding them shrimp, other people were waiting for you."

"Yes, sir."

"And you have nothing else to say?" he said shortly.

"No, sir."

He rolled his eyes back and waved at me to go away.

I went back on duty and finished my shift with no further disruptions in service, but more than a few odd looks from the other patrons.

Saul called me into his office after dinner was over and gave me what he called "the plain, unvarnished word."

"I expect you will treat all of the guests with the same level or service and respect. I don't know what transpired with you and the two ladies, but do not let it happen again."

"Yes, sir."

Katy caught up with me just as I left Saul's office. "Janice told me what happened. What were you thinking?"

"I wasn't. I was following the orders of a Mistress of Ay'esha. That's what I do."

She shook her head violently. "You can not just follow orders blindly. Everybody was staring at you. Now what do they think?"

"Was I supposed to care?" I asked, actually a bit uncertain.

"Serving a Mistress of Ay'esha privately or in a small group of the Daughters is one thing, but in a public place is another one entirely," she explained.

"But, if I don't make a habit of following the orders now, I might forget and make a mistake later," I objected.

She groaned in frustration. "I know it's been said that a male slave only has two brain cells, but I hoped you'd be the exception to the rule."

"I'm sorry. Am I being a bit too careful about serving properly?" I said.

"Yes, perhaps you are. None of the Mistresses here have the right to punish you for making a mistake. Only the Queen and I have the right to do that. And even when you return to your Mistress, she is the one who has the right to punish you. No one else," she said patiently.

I sighed in a mixture of relief and embarrassment. "Am I in trouble now?"

"No, silly. But there are a lot of people who are wondering what Janice and Amanda did to get you to do that."

"I was only following orders?"

XXIV

She sat in a corner during my fencing lesson and watched as I did my Errol Flynn imitation with Mrs. Hoffmann.

When we took a break, Mrs. Hoffmann suggested we change from fencing foils to sabers.

"I think it's time you changed to something a bit more challenging."

I was still a bit pumped up from the earlier practice, so I agreed. The saber was a bit heavier and it took a bit more wrist and a lot more control to handle it. The difference became very apparent in the first few minutes of practice and Mrs. Hoffmann demonstrated that by "killing" me multiple times.

"You need to keep the blade higher, Mr. Freeman," she said as she penetrated my defenses again.

I started becoming angry and my performance worsened even more.

A few minutes later she stepped back and lowered her sword. "Well, if someone attacks you with a saber, you die. We'll try with an épée tomorrow. That's a bit lighter and probably more controllable for you."

"I wish you had a katana blade. I think I'd actually do better with that," I said, hanging up my saber.

Mrs. Hoffmann looked at me intently. "I do. But, you do understand that I will bloody the blade before I put it away."

"If you can," I said confidently.

She smiled and left the gym.

"Are you crazy?" Katy asked, as I hung up my mask. "Bloody the blade?"

"Yes. You don't draw a katana blade without putting the blood of an enemy or your blood on the blade."

"No," she said.

"Excuse me?"

"No. I forbid it."

Mrs. Hoffmann walked back into the room at that point carrying two katana swords. "What were you forbidding him to do?"

"I don't want him using a real weapon. Someone could get hurt," Katy protested.

"He claims he can use one. A little blood will remind him not to be so cocky," she said, handing me one of the swords.

As I gripped the handle, all of my old training came into place again.

Katy stepped back from me as she saw the change in my demeanor.

I stood taller and more confidently. I knew I could do this. And I knew why I wanted to do this, even if Katy didn't.

Mrs. Hoffmann drew her blade as I drew mine.

We stared at each other for a moment and then as swift as a striking cobra, she swung. Without any conscious thought, I blocked her and parried, swinging the blade in a reverse action that caught her across the arm, cutting the fabric of her fencing jacket.

I turned and faced her and saw the anger in her build.

I stepped back and bowed to her in respect.

She paused, returned the bow and took up her position again.

This time, I took the offensive and feinted to her left.

She disregarded my feint and drove towards me, forcing me to turn and block. Her blade slipped by me as I turned. She swung backwards, and I fell back to avoid being slashed across the stomach.

I could sense her. All of the training of my Kendo master flowed back into me, a renewal of myself.

I saw Katy out of the corner of my eye as she watched the two of us.

A quick motion and the flash of the blade were blocked by mine with a ringing of steel.

"Should I do my Ben Kenobi imitation now?" I said, bowing again. "Or, would you like to do your Darth Vader?"

Mrs. Hoffmann raised her mask, and I saw her smile. It was the smile of a wolf about to devour a rabbit. "'Your powers are weak old man. You should not have come back.'"

"You mean I shouldn't have challenged you? Who else did you tell I was in the sauna?" I said holding my blade at the ready.

Her response was to slash forward with her blade, as I ducked and tripped her to the floor, kicking the blade from her hand.

Katy pounced on her and pinned her down as I got to my feet.

"Did you have anything to do with the incident in the sauna?" she demanded.

"No! I was talking with one of the guests about the facilities and mentioned the saunas. I did warn her that he was in one, so she wouldn't be startled."

"Who?"

She shook her head. "I don't know her. She's a new guest. I haven't seen her before."

Katy climbed off Mrs. Hoffmann, and I helped her to her feet. I helped Mrs. Hoffmann, handed her the katana, and held out my palm.

"Blood for your steel," I offered.

She raised her mask and drew the blade gently across my palm drawing a trickle of blood. Wiping the blade, she offered her hand to me for the same ritual drawing of blood.

I drew the blood from her, wiped my blade clean and bowed in respect to her.

She returned the bow, and we shook hands.

"You did have a good instructor. I enjoyed the challenge. You were very focused on things."

"I think so. The first time I caught him with a reversed blade he stopped, bowed, and than proceeded to treat me with more respect as a student," I said.

Katy apologized for her anger, and Mrs. Hoffmann just smiled. "Katy, it's nice to see you caring about someone that way. He can take care of himself in more ways than one."

"She's just a bit overprotective after what happened. If something happened to a guest and word got out, it could really be a problem for the Spa," I explained.

"Yes, dead bodies do have a tendency to draw attention. And I get the impression that you aren't the most popular person around here," she said lightly.

"You've noticed?" I said cheerfully.

Katy pulled me away before I could get myself in any deeper and we walked out.

She waited until we were away from the main building before she exploded. "On your knees, slave!"

I dropped and waited head down for my punishment.

"You took a chance doing that. I told you not to and you disobeyed me," she continued.

"Yes, Miss Katy. But I had to," I said.

"Why did you have to? Was it a case of macho insanity I witnessed?"

"Miss Katy, I needed to prove to myself that my time with Ay'esha hadn't destroyed the person inside me. That I still had the fire inside."

She said nothing, and I waited for the other shoe to drop. I had disobeyed a direct order from the superior present.

"Get up," she said, led me to the pool and hip checked me in.

I spluttered my way to the surface in anger. "What was that for?"

"You needed to cool off. A fire inside is good. Letting it escape is not."

Her smile cooled my anger, and I laughed. "Yes, Miss Katy. Noted and logged,"

She was right. I was trying to be a super slave. Not just be a good slave, but to be the ultimate slave.

Moderation is what Minx and Dr. Ruth had tried to instill in my mind, and I still hadn't learned.

"Why are you laughing?" she asked, reaching out to help me out of the pool.

I pulled her into the pool with me with a tremendous splash.

"Because, I just remembered something funny!" I said as she came to the surface. "I am remembering a lesson that Minx and Mei Ling taught me. I am a good slave, not the greatest, but a good one," I said.

"So?"

"So, I should concentrate on being a good one."

She grinned. "You are the strangest man I've ever met."

"I'm cute, though."

XXV

We were walking down the beach, wet, dumb and happy when I heard a cry for help from the water. In the lights from the restaurant patio, I could see a figure in the water waving his or her arms.

Katy ran for the water after telling me to run for help.

I ran up to the patio and grabbed a phone. "Neils, this is Charles. We've got someone in the water at the beach in trouble. Katy's gone in after them."

"Get back to the beach, I'm coming!" he said.

I ran back down to the beach in time to see Katy reach the figure and disappear into the crest of a wave. I waited for them to reappear. Seconds passed as I stood there watching. Then, two figures broke the surface for a moment and disappeared again into another wave.

They were getting farther out with each wave and the flailing was becoming weaker. I couldn't tell who was who any more.

I shifted from foot to foot nervously. Where the fuck was Neils?

I couldn't wait any longer and ran into the water towards the struggle. I swam as hard as I could towards the figures and saw in the reflected light that one of them was Amanda. She had her arms wrapped around Katy and kept pulling her down into the water, as Katy struggled to break the hold.

I pulled at Amanda's arms when she came to the surface again, and she released Katy and grabbed me.

"Gotcha," she said and pulled me to the bottom.

We must have been in about ten feet of water but it felt like ten miles worth as I tried to swim to the surface again. I regained the surface and saw Katy swimming towards me again. On the beach I saw lights pointed towards us.

"I'm trying to help you," I gasped.

"I'm not," she hissed and pulled me down again.

I went limp in her arms and my ears popped as she took me deeper into the water. I fought back the panic as my childhood accident bloomed in my mind.

I was at the lake on vacation high in the mountains. My sister was supposed to be watching me, but I'd slipped away on my own and waded into the water. A few feet into the lake, I dropped into a hole and sank to the bottom.

I thrashed my way to the surface and tried to call for help, but I sank again. I might have just been able to float to the surface, if I had remained calm, but like a wild animal, I clawed at the water engulfing me. I reached the surface again and cried out.

My sister heard me and dove into the water and pulled me up, as I was sinking for what would have been the last time and dragged me to shore.

"You are a stupid boy, Michael," she screamed in fear and anger, as I cried.

She took me home and for the rest of that summer. I couldn't even look at the lake without crying. A few months later I cried again as they lowered her coffin into the ground. She had crashed her car coming home from the city with my birthday present. She was nineteen years old.

I held my breath as long as I could. I heard the sounds of thrashing in the water, and then felt myself being dragged towards the surface again.

I popped to the surface and gulped in air again, as Neils pulled Amanda and me apart.

She kicked him in the face and tried to pull me down again, only this time I had enough time to grab the rescue buoy that Neils swam out with and stayed on the surface.

She released me and dove for the bottom as Katy swam up and

grabbed the float as well.

Neils started to go after her, but I called him back. "Let her go. I'll explain later."

He looked at the spot where she had disappeared and then joined us, as we swam back to shore.

All the while I kept looking over my shoulder for Amanda to surface like Jaws and try and attack again.

XXVI

Neils wasn't exactly happy with being told to forget what he'd seen and was a bit concerned about Amanda washing up on the beach dead.

"Neils, I wouldn't worry. She swims like a fish. The drowning bit was just her way of getting to me," I said, sipping a hot cup of tea in the kitchen.

"Why is what I don't understand," he said worriedly.

"Well, she hit on me, and I turned her down. I don't fool around," I said, glancing at Katy for a little help.

"She must really be disturbed," he said.

"In more ways than one," Katy said darkly.

And that closed the incident so far as Neils was concerned.

Katy on the other hand was not content to let things "sleep with the fishes." When we got back to my room she ordered me to strip and kneel, face on the floor, and not move until she returned.

I did and waited, knowing that I had really pushed the outside of the envelope, as Chuck Yeager would put it, with my actions. I hadn't disobeyed an order, but I had certainly put myself at risk.

But I'm a bit stupid that way. Katy was in danger of drowning, and I couldn't just stand there. Neils knew where I was going, so I didn't think I was taking that much of a risk.

When Katy returned, I could see she was wearing high heels but that was all I could see from my position.

"Do not move, slave," she said closing the door.

I held my position even as the lights went out. I became nervous as I knelt there. Could Katy be one of the people trying to kill me? I fought with my fears in the dark. What was she doing in the darkness that filled the room? I could hear her moving and then a click of a lighter.

Slowly the room filled with flickering candlelight.

"Are you ready for your punishment?" she asked from behind me.

"Yes, Miss Katy," I answered.

I heard a whir and the felt the solid crack of a cane across my exposed ass. I whimpered.

"One!" she said.

Again, the sound and the pain.

"Two!"

And yet again.

I moaned from the blow and gasped for breath.

"Three!"

A pause and I felt her hand on my punished flesh, running a finger across the weals.

"You will start obeying properly after this, won't you?" she said with a sharp edge in her voice.

"Yes, Miss Katy," I moaned.

The hand was removed and I felt the slash of the cane again even harder, collapsing me to the floor.

"I don't believe you. You haven't obeyed properly yet. You persist in doing things your way, without asking for permission or advice. You try to be a good slave, and you do very well most of the time. But, you risked your life tonight twice without regard for your Mistress's feelings or mine."

She was right.

"I will protect you, as will the Queen. Your insistence on protecting yourself without help is disrespectful and shows a lack of trust in us. You will trust us, as you do your Mistress, to protect and care for you, or I will recommend that you be returned to your Mistress as a failure."

I lay there and listened to her words, stinging me more than the cane ever could. I wanted to protest, to tell her she was wrong. I couldn't. She was right. I had grown so accustomed to having to take care of myself, that when the time came for someone to care for me, I couldn't accept it.

I had to be a man about it. What a crock of shit. Mistress Minx loved me and cared for me. I accepted that. Why couldn't I accept that other people might also love and care for me as well?

I had isolated myself after my wife and daughter died. I stuck to my work, didn't socialize. My friends and I grew apart. I didn't do anything except go to work and come home to my empty house. When Denise died, all of the love in the world and all of the love I had for the world died, as well. I punished myself for failing to save her.

If I had just kept driving that night, not stopping to help someone in distress, I would never have been brought to Ay'esha. My life would have continued in the same vein until I died. Alone and forgotten.

I started to weep at my foolishness and pride. I would never have been forgiven.

Mistress Minx. I wanted to be with her so badly at that moment.

"Your Mistress does love you, or she would not have sent you here. You are a very special man."

I didn't say anything. There was nothing to say.

And that is how I spent that night. Lying on the floor, thinking about my foolish pride and Minx's love for me.

The next morning, Katy said nothing to me about the incident at all. She had slept while I had lain awake on the floor.

My muscles protested as I took my shower, and the soap caused the welts on my ass to burn, but not as much as the embarrassment did.

The morning jog on the beach was a bit easier as Katy ran with me instead of riding on me. There was a bit of a chill in our relationship that hurt as much as the cane did, but I tried to keep my focus on the tasks at hand.

We passed Ms. Claire on the way to the gym, and I greeted her politely.

She ignored me and continued toward the pool without a backward glance.

"Well, I guess she didn't have anything to do with last night's little fiasco, or she's a damned fine actress," I speculated.

Katy ignored the comment, and when we got to the gym, we found Mistress Janice working out. "Good morning, children!"

I knelt before her for a pat on the head, and she looked down at me and then back at the expression on Katy's face.

"I see that you two have a little problem today. Is there anything I can do to help?"   "Yes. Would you keep an eye on him for a little while? I need to speak to Mrs. Queen about something. When he's finished his exercises, perhaps you could go to breakfast with him?" asked Katy.

"Of course, dear. I'll take good care of him," Mistress Janice assured her.

Katy left, and I started my usual workout routine. I had increased my weightlifting abilities during my stay and was actually leg pressing over three hundred pounds. Looking at the scales, I grimaced. I should have used my legs as a brace and just forced the door open instead of breaking the glass. Oh, well, 20/20 hindsight.

Mistress Janice just watched as I went from machine to machine, saying nothing, but noticing my distraction.

"Charles, stop what you're doing and come here."

I walked back to where she was sitting on a weight bench and knelt before her.

She patted the bench and invited me to sit next to her. "Now, tell me all about it. What happened between you and Katy?"

"I'm not sure I should talk about it, Mistress," I said.

"I can make it an order you know," she smiled. "Now, what's the problem?"

"I'm not a very good slave sometimes, and Katy had to punish me. I think she thinks she's not a very good Mistress because I screwed up," I confessed.

Mistress Janice hugged me for a moment before speaking. "I know Mistress Minx by her reputation. She is a very demanding Mistress, because she doesn't want a groveling worm for a slave. She wants a slave who can stand up for himself and takes pride in serving her. Someone who wants to serve her, not someone who has to serve her to feel complete.

"Katy is still young and learning her way. She has never felt like a Mistress of Ay'esha, although she is one in her spirit. Her way is not the same as Mistress Minx's or my way. My slaves want to serve me, because I love them and care for them."

"But, I don't know what would make Katy happy. I'm just trying to learn what I was sent here to learn. I don't want her blaming herself if I'm not a good slave," I protested.

"That is not something you can control. All you can do is attempt to follow her orders as well as you can."

"It's pretty hard not to try and control it."

"That's called Topping from the Bottom. Not a really good idea," she warned.

"Yes, Mistress."

"It's Janice, unless I tell you otherwise. Let's go eat."

XXVII

I guess Katy must have left orders for my breakfast, because before I could order, the server said she knew what I wanted.

Janice found that amusing, as she ordered her breakfast. "She keeps you on a pretty tight leash, doesn't she?"

"I wish she didn't at times. I'd love to have some hash browns," I complained.

"She's just watching out for you. Just like your wife did," she said, sipping her juice.

"Excuse me?" I said carefully.

"Oh, I know you're married, or at least were. I can tell from the way you act around other women. Willing to please them, but not anxious about it. And, I can see where your ring was worn."

"If you don't mind telling me, how did you learn to be that observant?"

"Oh, I've been around a long time. I make jewelry, so I have a habit of looking at people's hands. The rest, well, just experience," she demurred.

The food arrived, but instead of the usual dry cereal and toast, I was served a small steak and hash browns.

"Excuse me, I don't think this is my order," I said.

"No, Miss Katy said to feed you meat today. Enjoy it," the server said and went on her way.

Well, in the words of Gomer Pyle, "Surprise, surprise, surprise."

"I'm not sure if this is a test or not," I said looking at the food.

"Well, do you think she'd try and trick you into violating an order?" Janice asked.

"I'm not sure. But I'm not going to take any chances today."

I called the server and had her take the food away and bring me my normal breakfast.

I watched with regret the departure of the hash browns, but I knew that I would be better off eating my corn flakes.

Katy came in a few minutes later and joined us.

She didn't say anything about the steak, and I didn't say anything at all.

Janice excused herself after a few minutes, ostensibly to use the ladies room, but I think Katy and I both knew better.

We both started to speak at the same time and stopped.

"You first Miss Katy," I offered.

"No, you go ahead," she said.

"I want to apologize for disappointing you. I haven't been on my best behavior."

"And I wanted to apologize for taking my disappointment out on you," she said.

"Friends?" I asked, holding out my hand.

"No. Master and servant," she said shaking her head.

"Yes, Miss Katy," I said withdrawing my hand.

"That would be 'Yes, Mistress Katherine', if you please."

I smiled in relief. "Yes Mistress Katherine."

Janice returned to the table to find me feeding Mistress Katherine grapes from her fruit cup.

"I see you two are back to normal," she said happily.

"No, ma'am. Better than before," I corrected.

My time at the Spa seemed to speed along with the change in Mistress Katherine's attitude. There were no other incidents, and I was soon permitted to roam freely again.

Jerry Dodge taught me how to at least sit on a horse, but I never did learn to ride very well. Neils taught me how to swim much better and even gave me some basic scuba lessons with Mistress Katherine's help.

People came, and people went. Ms. Claire departed a few days after Amanda disappeared and Miss Judy extended her stay an extra week. Before she left, Mistress Janice praised me to the Queen and Mistress Katherine, and I finally did learn how to cut a tomato properly.

Even Mr. Terwilliger got off my back as soon as I admitted I wanted to learn the piano.

His "Happy Fingers" exercise stank, but I did discover I could at least play "Chopsticks."

Which he hated.

Weeks passed. Mistress Minx had said only two weeks. What had happened to her?

One morning after my exercise, I was called to the Queen's office. I knelt before her as she picked up a report.

"You have applied yourself well after the early part of your stay here. You are in far better physical shape than you were before, and your mental attitude has improved as well."

"Thank you, Ma'am," I said humbly.

"Yes," she said reading the report. "There is only one problem you need to work on."

I waited. What was I still doing wrong?

"You need to be a little less aggressive in how you do things. Willingness is good, and being intent is good. But, you do have a problem with getting either too focused on a problem or not seeing the big picture.

"The things you do and the choices you make reflect on your Mistress and on Ay'esha. Always remember that."

"Yes, Ma'am."

She walked around her desk, sat on the edge of it and looked down at me. "Have you considered what you're going to do when you leave here?"

The question startled me. Leave? "I expected to serve Mistress Minx again. I hadn't really thought about anything else."

The Queen shook her head. "No, I mean for a living. What kind of work do you want to do?"

"I was trained to solve computer problems, Ma'am. And I've

learned how to solve people problems here. I'm not sure what I would do," I said honestly.

"Think about it," she said and turned away.

"Ma'am?" I asked.

"Yes, slave?"

"Is something wrong? Have I done something to offend you?" I asked seriously.

She turned back and laughed. "No, slave. But your time in training is finished. You're going home."

XXVIII

Home. Where was my home now? I had begun to think of Minx's rooms at Ay'esha as home, but that was taken from me. Then, I had settled here. That was to be taken from me, as well.

I sat in my room and considered my fate.

The room grew dark as night came. What was I going to do? Was I going to see Mistress Minx again? Had I been abandoned? No. That, I knew in my heart. She said she would never leave me.

A knock on the door stirred me from my thoughts.

"Come in!" I called.

Mistress Katherine opened the door and switched on the lights. "Why are you sitting in the dark?"

"I'm sorry, Mistress. I just didn't feel like turning on the lights."

She sat on the bed next to me and put her hand on my leg. "Are you all right?"

I turned to her. "No I am not all right. I'm confused and hurt and even a little bit angry."

"About what?"

"I don't know what's going on. I'm told I'm a slave of Ay'esha, but then I'm told I'm going home. I don't even know if I have a home to go to anymore. I'm not sure what's going on."

"Michael, it's time for you to leave the nest. That's what's going on," she said softly.

"That's the first time you've ever called me by my proper name,"

I said in wonder.

"I've known all along. But Charles Freeman doesn't exist anymore. Michael Forbin is going out into the real world again. And the Michael I know is strong and proud and healthy and able to take care of himself."

"It's been a long time. In fact I don't even really know how long. I didn't even have an idea of the date until I got here," I said.

"Do you want to know how long you've been gone?" she asked.

I hesitated.

"Yes."

"You have been in the control of Ay'esha for almost a year."

My mouth fell open. "I've been gone a year?"

"Almost. And in that time you have been reborn. It takes nine months for cow or countess to have a child. Why should it take any less time for a slave to be born?" she said reasonably.

"I know but --"

"Michael, listen to me. You will understand everything soon. But come with me now. There is something you need to see," she said, rising and holding her hand out to me.

She led me to the beach and there, waiting on the sand, was a meal.

"Eat with me one last time, Michael. Tomorrow you return to whence you came."

We ate in silence and watched the moon rise over the water, turning it into a show of sparkling light.

It was comforting somehow, despite the emotions in my heart, to see it. I knew that somehow Mistress Minx was watching over me, and the moonlight fell gently upon me like a blessing from my Goddess.

"Thank you," I finally said to Mistress Katherine.

"The sea and the light are always comforting to a troubled soul. They are eternal and we are not," she said.

"Time and tide wait for no man," I said remembering the old poem.

"No, they do not. And the tides of our lives take up to places we have never seen or imagined. And when the time comes to leave, we do."

She looked at me, her face glowing softly in the moonlight. "You are a fine man, Michael, and you have taught me things, as well. Someday, we may meet again."

She kissed me, and I felt a weariness come over me. I looked out over the water, and it seemed to blur in the light into a dazzle. And then, nothing.

XXIX

The alarm clock woke me up, I rolled over and almost fell on the floor. I slapped it off and sat up, startled.

I didn't have an alarm clock in my room. I hadn't had a clock since before I was taken by Minx.

I was in my bed. In my house.

This was impossible. Or, was it? Had I dreamed the whole thing? Minx, Ay'esha, Lydia, all specters of my mind.

I felt like Scrooge the next morning. I looked out the window and saw my car parked in the driveway.

I got out of bed and made my way into the living room.

The room was clean and orderly, cleaner than I usually left it. A stack of mail was piled on the desk, and when I went into the kitchen, I found food in the cabinets and fresh milk in the fridge.

I opened the door and found the newspaper waiting for me as it always had been.

The date confirmed that it had been a little over nine months since that night.

So, I had been gone. Or, was the headline a joke? Did someone have it printed for this occasion?

I switched on the TV and found out that cable was still connected. I switched to the Weather Channel, and the date indicated on the screen matched the newspaper.

It finally occurred to look at myself in the mirror.

The body I looked at was not the body I had left the house in.

It was the body developed over the months with Mistress Minx and the Queen.

I was home. My mind spun. If I were home, where was Mistress Minx? Would I see her again?

My medallion was gone.

The confusion was even worse now.

I picked up the phone and called my office. The number was disconnected.

I got dressed in the clothing I found in the closet. It all fit, so someone had been there and replaced all of my old clothes.

I found my car keys in the bowl on the table where I always kept them and got into the car. It had a full tank of gas and the mileage reading showed that the car had been used by someone.

I drove towards my office, and as I reached the place where I had first seen Minx, I pulled over and parked.

There was no sign of anything in that spot, not even an oil stain.

I finished driving to town and looked at all the changes that had happened during my absence.

Things seemed newer and different. One change was my office. There was a FOR SALE sign on the property, and no sign that the company ever existed.

I drove back home and parked.

Opening the front door, I found an envelope on the floor marked with my name.

I opened it and my medallion fell out with a note.

My loving slave,

I know you are confused and perhaps a bit frightened by what has happened.

Please trust me when I say we will be reunited someday. You will find things as you left them, perhaps a bit better than they were when we met.

Always remember that I love you,

The signature was that of my Mistress.

And so, the lost lamb had come home.

XXX

"The years go faster than the days, there's no warmth in the light,

"Where we spent our last few days, Benson's on my mind."

Well, Benson wasn't exactly on my mind, but where we spent our last few days kept surfacing in my memories.

I was still getting used to being at home in my own bed after the months I spent inside of Ay'esha. Mistress Minx had promised never to leave me, but in those first few days, I wondered if I was fooling myself.

I discovered that my bills had been paid during my absence from a bank account, now closed, that had belonged to L. Minelli. Even my taxes had been done. I was impressed by Ay'esha's abilities to cover up my absence and wondered how many people had simply disappeared.

I had sorted through all of the mail that had piled up during my absence, and found nothing of real interest at all. Just copies of paid bills and more bills.

My first priority was to find a job. My old company had gone bankrupt, and I was using the savings in my account to cover the day-to-day expenses.

The first problem I ran into was explaining the nine month absence in my work record. The explanation of a long vacation didn't impress many employers, and I soon found myself doing temp work to keep things going.

My first temp job was simple enough, installing computer

hardware for an aerospace company. It paid decently, but I was bored and kept looking for other work.

Every night, as I drove home, I slowed down near the spot where I had first seen Minx, the night she took me from the world. But every night my headlights flashed on the same empty place I had found the first time I looked.

The time passed slowly, and I soon began to give up on the idea of seeing Mistress Minx again. Perhaps, I wasn't as good a slave as I had thought, and she had given up on me. She had told me when we first bonded that the time would come when we would have to separate. I had accepted that at the time, but with each lonely night, my resolve weakened.

Perhaps I was searching for the equivalent of Brigadoon, a place that only appeared once every hundred years.

Thanksgiving came and went, and then Christmas came.

And with it, a Christmas miracle.

I was watching "A Christmas Carol" on TV and thinking how much my life had been like that of Scrooge until Mistress Minx came into it. I had gotten into the spirit enough where I had purchased a tree and decorated it for the first time in many a year.

Presents from my coworkers were piled under it, a welcome change from previous years, and I had begun to rebuild old friendships long neglected. I had even begun to date a young woman I had met on the job, not seriously, but dinner on occasion.

I must have dozed off, because when I awoke, there was a silver-wrapped box under the tree that hadn't been there before.

The movie had gone off and all there was on the screen was static, making a hissing noise that reminded me of surf on the beach.

I turned off the set, and I could hear the staccato pitter patter of rain on the roof that Christmas Eve.

"I almost wish it were snow," I thought walking towards the box that had appeared.
Perhaps my friend Kim had crept in and left it to surprise me.

The card on the box was addressed to M-5.

My hands shook, as I lifted the box and shook it gingerly. I heard something moving, something light but solid.

My eyes filled with tears as I opened it and found on a bed of tissue paper the collar that Mistress Minx had given me almost a year before. It was closed to symbolize our bond and my name tag hung from the loop on it.

I picked it up, and as I did so, a note fell on the floor. It was a stanza from Lewis Carroll.

"The time has come the Walrus said, to talk of many things
 Of shoes and ships and sealing wax, of cabbages and kings
"And why the sea is boiling hot, and whether pigs have wings."

As I read it, I heard a noise from outside, the sound of a car door slamming. I threw open the front door in time to see a large car pull away from the curb with its lights off.

I ran to the curb calling for the unseen driver to wait, but it was too late, and the car had passed from sight.

"No, not this time," I swore and ran to my car.

It started easily for a change, and I backed out of the driveway and set out in pursuit of my nighttime visitor. They couldn't have gotten too far ahead of me, I told myself that rainy Christmas Eve. I was determined to catch them.

Ten minutes later, I conceded that they had escaped. I never saw the car again that evening. It had vanished into that cold rain like the spirit of Christmas Past.

I slept that night, collar in hand. I could not bear to place it around my neck; only Mistress Minx could do that for me.

That Christmas morning I puzzled over the note. I read it over and over again seeking a hidden meaning to it. Nothing came to mind.

I had Christmas dinner with Kim and her family that night. It was quite a nice dinner, and I had managed to put off thinking about my visitor for a short while. We had reached the coffee stage of the meal when the subject of my past arose.

Kim's father was a good natured man in his fifties, but very much the type of man who wanted only the best for his daughter.

"I understand from Kim that you are a widower," he said, casually.

"Dad!" Kim interposed.

"No, it's fine, dear," I said. "Yes, I am."

"Have you ever considered getting married again? You're still a young man," he continued.

I rose from my chair and faced him. "Sir, I enjoy the company of your daughter. She has been a very good friend to me. But I have no interest in marrying her or anybody else at this time."

He looked at me and scowled, "And your reasons? If you don't mind my asking."

"I don't mind your asking. I do mind you asking me in front of your daughter. I am not in love with your daughter."

As I said it, I realized it was true. I still loved my wife, and I loved Mistress Minx.

Kim looked at me sadly as I said the words, but I knew she understood. "Dad, leave it alone. What made you think I want to marry him?"

"Kim, honey. You're not a little girl any more. It's time you got married, started a family."

Kim rolled her eyes skyward. "Dad, is this the 'I want grandchildren speech again'?"

"Kim--"

She turned to me and apologized. "Michael, I'm sorry about this. My father is up to his old tricks playing matchmaker again."

"I'm sorry, too. But, better I should tell you now. I'm in love with someone gone from this world," I said softly. "Good night."

As I walked out, Kim followed me and took my hand. "Friends?"

"Always," I smiled, kissing her.

As I drove home, I considered things. Was it foolish to be in love with a woman I could never have? Or, perhaps that's why I did love her. She was safe to love, because I could never have her.

I didn't sleep well that night. I dreamt of Minx and Mei Ling. Of the night I saw them make love to each other. And in my dreams I saw Denise. My wife, gone to the Goddess. And she smiled at me in my dreams and forgave me. The two dreams mixed and became as one. Denise and Minx making love to Mei Ling, and then Denise making love to me as Minx watched and smiled with Mei Ling's arms around her.

I woke with a start to the sound of the telephone ringing. It was well past my usual time to get up, and I could see the rain falling again through the bedroom window.

Before I could answer it, the phone stopped and I lay there for a moment.

I could still see the dream clearly and marveled at myself for being able to recall it. Then, I realized that I couldn't recall the name of the town the Spa was in. I could remember the people and the place, but I couldn't remember the location of it.

What else was missing from my memories? I got out of bed and took my shower and tried to think, searching my mind for blank spots. And if I found any, would I actually know about it? Had I ever known?

A truly 1984-ish paradox. What had gone down the memory hole? Almost the Zen question of the butterfly. Am I a butterfly dreaming that I am a man, or a man dreaming I am a butterfly?

Oh, well. I shaved in the shower as usual and wrapped my robe around me. Many things had been removed from my closet during my absence, and it relieved me that my robe was still there, threadbare and worn.

Denise had given me that robe the second Christmas we were together, and she had worn it the day I took her to the hospital, never to return. It took me a long time before I could look at it or wear it again without thinking of that last trip.

I tied the cord against the chill of the room and went into the kitchen to make coffee, passing the desk and the answering machine as I did so. I hit the playback button and heard the rumbles and twirps of the voice in reverse, and the message played back.

"This is the Anderson Agency calling. If you are still looking for a job, give us a call," said an unidentified woman's voice. The voice gave me the number, repeated it twice, and then before the message ended, I could hear in the background a piece of music.

"White Rabbit."

Curiouser and curiouser . Two references to Lewis Carroll in as many days. Something was going on.

When I went into the yard to pick up the paper, I was tempted to look in the tree for a smile without a cat.

I ate my breakfast while scanning the paper for anything that caught my attention in the help wanted ads. Nothing of any real interest.

I decided to call the number on the machine and see what they wanted.

"Anderson Agency," a voice said.

"Yes, this is Michael Forbin. Someone called earlier today and left a message for me," I said.

There was a rustle of papers.

"I'm sorry, but I don't have any record of a call to you. Do you know the name of the person who called you?"

I started to say no, but then I had a flash of inspiration.

"I think it was Alice," I said confidently.

"One moment."

There was a long pause before I heard a voice again.

"This is Alice. How may I help you?"

"Alice, this is Michael Forbin. You left a message about a job earlier today for me," I said.

There was a shortish pause.

"I left a message today, yes. I'm not sure I was leaving it for you." She repeated a phone number.

"Yes, that's my number," I confirmed. "Can you tell me what all of the cloak and dagger stuff is about?"

"Can I have your social security number, please?"

I recited it and again asked her what the call was all about.

"Have you had a close encounter with something unusual in the last twelve months?"

I wanted to scream I was so tense, but managed to control myself enough to answer.

"Yes I have," I said tightly. Was this my ticket back to Ay'esha? Or was this a ticket into the clutches of Lydia?

"Thank you. One moment."

I waited with a racing heart.

"I'm sorry, Mr. Forbin. The client insisted on these conditions before discussing the job offer."

"Did those conditions also include playing White Rabbit?" I asked.

"Yes. I'm not sure why," Alice said," In any case, if you are interested in a new job, I have a package to send to you."

"Well, I'm interested all right."

That was an understatement.

"Fine, I'll send the package to you, and you can contact the client directly," she said, confirmed my mailing address and hung up.

That call did me a lot of good. I didn't know anything more that I did before the call. Other than the fact it involved a job offer and a mysterious client with a subtle sense of humor. The whole call was a test to see how smart I was. Was Mistress Minx behind it? And, why the secret agent routine? She could just call me and tell me where to go and when and I would.

That is if it was Minx and not Lydia.

Three anxious days later the package arrived. The job I was being offered was at a large financial institution in a large city north of the place I lived in. I would be assisting the Chief Financial Officer and some international travel would be involved. The letter hinted that the job was a difficult one and that the majority of applicants failed the interview.

The reasons for my selection were not given, just that I had been recommended highly.

The package included a set of airline tickets for the flight to the city and hotel reservations in my name for a two night stay.

Well, I figured that if they wanted to pick up the tab, the least I could do was to go to the interview. I wasn't sure I wanted the job, or could even do the job, but an all expense paid trip?

All right, let's go.

I called the number in the package and reached a voice mail system. I left a message confirming my interest, and that I would be there at the stated day and time for my interview.

If it were Lydia, she was going to a lot of trouble to get to me.

But the collar and the note comforted me.

The time had come.

It was a very nervous Michael Forbin that boarded the plane that day. I had my bag and my briefcase. And packed away in the bag was my collar. Just for good luck.

Although, explaining it to the airport security officers was a bit unnerving. They accepted my story that it was a gift for a friend and with knowing winks, they let me pass.

I studied the landscape below as we flew. My seat companion was a heavy set man who snored and took up more than his share of the armrest. I tried to focus on the interview. Perhaps it didn't have anything to do with Minx or Lydia or Ay'esha, at all. My reputation as a problem solver was known from my earlier work. Perhaps that's who suggested me for this job.

The speculation came to a halt the next morning.

My night in the hotel had been a restless one. I kept dreaming of Minx being tortured until she screamed in terror. Near sunrise I gave up and got out of bed. I dressed in casual clothes and left the hotel, walking along the quiet streets of the city. My path took me towards the waterfront and a large shopping area.

Even at this early hour, shops were beginning to open. The fish markets with their bounty from the sea. A bakery with fresh bread. Its aroma flowing into the streets. I stood on the end of the pier and watched the sun creep over the horizon. Maybe I was chasing a dream, but I had thought my dreams were lost forever.

After breakfast in a cafe on the pier, I returned to the hotel and got cleaned up and dressed for the interview. I didn't know who I was going to work for, but I wanted to look perfect, no matter how nervous I was about things.

Some people get butterflies in their stomachs. I get pterodactyls in mine. My nerves got more of a workout when I reached the location for the interview. It was the largest building in that part of town and the busiest.

I entered it, reminding myself that they had called me, and I was expected. That and the fact I was Mistress Minx's slave, her pride and joy, kept me upright and stable.

The interview started quite well. Before I could say much on anything, the HR director, Mrs. Cabazon, slid the offer across the polished wood table.

I looked at the figures and then at Mrs. Cabazon. "Are you serious about these numbers?"

She nodded. "I consider it hazardous duty pay."

"Seriously, is this person that hard to work for?"

"I've already had to replace her assistants three times this year. Ms. Dawes just burns them out with her demands."

"Well, I get along with just about everybody. I'd like to interview with her at least."

The HR director shook her head. "You were warned. Just take the elevator. Her office is on the top floor."

"Just one question. Is she any relation to the owners of the bank?"

"Her family founded it."

Oh, shit. Spoiled rich girl in a family business. Probably propped up by Daddy's money and the skills of her assistant. It looked like I was just going to wind up being the scapegoat for her fuck ups from my point of view.

I took the elevator and considered how to approach Ms. Dawes. The door opened, and the receptionist directed me to the office at the end of the hall.

"She's expecting you. Just knock and enter."

I walked down the hallway to the door and took a deep breath.

"M. Dawes chief financial officer," the sign said.

Well, she was M. Dawes, but I was Michael Forbin. I was that good and that competent. I knocked firmly and entered, as I had been directed.

I looked around the office and didn't see any sign of the mysterious M. Dawes.

I could see most of the city out of the windows that lined the office. The desk was clean enough to land an airplane on and as black as night. A computer terminal sat on a small stand next to the main desk, and I could see the constant flow of information reflected in the polished wood of the desk.

A large chair was behind the desk, its back turned towards me blocking my view of the occupant. All I could see were the legs and feet.

I waited silently for a moment and cleared my throat.

There was no reaction from the seated figure, so I walked up to the desk and started to speak again.

The chair turned and Mistress Minx just looked up at me.

I dropped to my knees before her, weeping in joy.

"Welcome home, Michael," she said, touching my face gently.

I couldn't speak at all, as she stroked my head and comforted me.

This was a Mistress Minx I did not know and had never suspected existed.

"What happened?" I finally asked when I could stop crying.

"Nothing happened, Michael. I just didn't need you until now. And you needed to reestablish yourself in the world again. I understand that you have even been dating. I'm very pleased."

"How long?" I started to ask.

"Oh, I've been watching you since you were returned to your own home. I took a risk in leaving that gift myself, but I had to."

"Why?"

She smiled at me gently. "Because, I love you Michael, and I wanted to see you. You needed a little reassurance of my love, so I left you the gift. I was sure that you would figure out the clues and find me."

"Mistress, I'm sorry. My faith in you wavered," I confessed.

"I understand that. I hadn't intended to be away that long. I told you that Lydia leaving Ay'esha would have an effect. It did, and I have been very busy. I intended to bring you directly here after you left the Spa, but the time was not yet right."

I nodded.

"Lydia's influence has poisoned many in Ay'esha, and those that can be trusted now are limited. She and her followers have disappeared from sight, but like the unseen shark, they may appear at any time, destroying and killing."

I sighed, thinking of the chaos I had caused in the name of love.

"You are blaming yourself again for something beyond your control," she said looking into my eyes.

"If I hadn't," I started to say, before she placed a finger on my lips.

"It would have happened anyway. It had to happen for Ay'esha to grow. We had become complacent, watching the world and controlling it from behind the scenes. Now we must be more proactive, take some risks to accomplish our goals. And keeping Lydia and her followers at bay is important. Their impulsive actions may reveal our plans to the world before the time is right."

"I understand," I said.

"Do you really? I hope so, because I have a place for you in all this."

My heart leapt. "What would please you, my Mistress?"

"The Mother of Many and I want you to start telling the world about Ay'esha, in your own words."

"I'm afraid I don't understand, Mistress."

"Michael, you have a rare gift. You are a story teller. Not merely a writer, but a story teller. You involve people in your stories and your jokes. You don't lecture to them; you invite them in. And, that is what we need now. Someone to tell the tales."

"But, what should I write about? I mean, what can I say?"

"Tell the stories of your life in Ay'esha. Express your feelings and your fears, your dreams and your hopes. I will help you, and so will the Mother of Many. We'll make sure you don't say too much. And when people read the stories, they may understand our purpose."

I was beginning to grasp my place in her world.

"As Lydia and her people try and destroy, we will need someone to tell the tales to balance it."

I knelt before her thinking of the task ahead. It would be a monumental job. To try and put on paper what I only felt in my heart and soul, to try and explain how and why. "Mistress, I'm not sure I can. I can tell the stories, but I'm not much of a writer."

She just stroked my head, letting me struggle with the indecision.

Perhaps she was right. I could tell the stories. Perhaps someone would gain from my mistakes.

"Would it please you, Mistress?" I asked.

"Yes, it would. And, it would be a great service to Ay'esha."

I looked into her eyes for the first time since our reunion. "Yes, Mistress. I will write the stories. But, who will read them?"

"There are always people looking for something beyond their lives. Those people will find your stories. Those who believe will contact us or make themselves known. Others will dismiss your stories as fantasy."

I looked down at the floor for a moment and then back at my beloved Mistress Minx, Minx the Controller. As always, she was correct. The stories deserved to be told. Surrendering to her, I jotted down the title, *The Diaries of Ay'esha: Trapped and Trained.*

ABOUT THE AUTHOR

Charles Forbin has been involved in the D/s scene since his mid-teens, has worked with some of the famous Dommes of the 70's and 80's, and is currently in service to a now retired Professional Dominatrix in Los Angeles.

When he is not serving his Mistress, he is a collector of movie soundtracks and obscure science fiction films of the last fifty years.

His works have been translated into multiple languages for the European market, and this is his first publication in the United States.

www.ingramcontent.com/pod-product-compliance
Lightning Source LLC
Chambersburg PA
CBHW071215260626
47162CB00004B/1303